ATHENA'S CHILD

HANNAH LYNN

sourcebooks
landmark

Published by Sourcebooks Landmark, an imprint of Sourcebooks
P.O. Box 4410, Naperville, Illinois 60567-4410
(630) 961-3900
sourcebooks.com

Originally published as *Athena's Child* in 2021 in the United Kingdom by Hannah Lynn.
This edition issued based on the paperback edition published in 2021 by Hannah Lynn.

Cataloging-in-Publication Data is on file with the Library of Congress.

Printed and bound in the United States of America.
VP 10 9 8 7 6 5 4 3 2 1

FOR THOSE WHOSE TRUTH HAS BEEN LOST,
MAY IT ONE DAY BE FOUND.

PROLOGUE

S OME BELIEVE THAT MONSTERS ARE BORN MONSTERS.

That some creatures arrive on this earth with a darkness so all-consuming in their hearts that no mere mortal's love could ever hope to tame it. These souls, they believe, cannot achieve redemption and do not deserve it. They are beasts, intent on causing chaos for all who cross their paths. They are vengeful and hate-filled, deserving of nothing except our contempt.

Perhaps it is true. Perhaps all monsters are born. Then again, perhaps it is just a way of hiding the darkness we all carry within us. A darkness we force ourselves to keep hidden from the world, for we can barely imagine what terrible misdoings would occur if we were to let that darkness grow. Because the truth that we all know is this. Darkness grows.

It would be easier if it did not. This story, in many ways, would be easier if the darkness had been born in her that way. But it was not. She was not. Medusa grew from monsters, but she was not born of them.

PART I

ONE

THE THREE FIGURES STOOD IN THE DOORWAY WATCHING THE flurries of dust bloom in the air. The silence that surrounded them was not an easy silence. It was a silence burdened with contemplation, of an unspoken question to which each one of them knew the answer but none would be the first to say.

The green of spring had been lost to the heat of summer. Long shadows of cypress trees marked out lines in the dry, powdery earth, and the smell of overripe fruit sweetened the air around them. Shriveled berries littered the ground, making glorious feasts for the insects that scurried over the rocks and dirt. Despite the sun having already begun its descent, the evening air was still heavy with the day's humidity. As the family stood watching the horse and rider disappear over the horizon, sweat wove its way down their brows and backs.

"We should consider it," said the mother, Aretaphila. It was always going to be she who was the first to speak. Her words were blunt and void of emotion, as if the matter were nothing more than a transaction, a sale at the market, which, of course, it was. To pretend it was more than that would be nothing short of foolish.

"We should not. We *will* not." Thales's eyes met his wife's for the first time since their visitor's departure.

"We can't keep delaying. We are fortunate. This is a good match."

"On what evidence do you make this claim?" Thales's voice hardened.

"I do have some experience in these matters," Aretaphila replied. The pair looked at the girl between them.

"Go inside," Aretaphila said to her firstborn. "Find your sisters. Make sure they have not made a mess of their clothes. And there will be no need to worry about cooking tonight. We have more than enough from our guest to make do."

Medusa's eyes moved from the horizon. With a simple, elegant nod to her mother, she turned to go.

"But take that thing off first." Her father motioned to the jewels wrapped around her neck. Medusa raised her hand and touched the necklace. Without so much as a word, she slipped the glimmering string of gemstones over her head and handed it to her father before disappearing inside.

The man on the horse had been the third visitor they had received in a month and the wealthiest by far. He had brought with him baskets of figs, wine, olives, meat, and jewelry. The necklace was embedded with gold and more garnet than any of them had seen in their lifetimes. Selling it would earn them more than their farm would in three years. Thales glanced down at the object and shuddered.

"Aretaphila," he said, taking his wife's hand in his. "What do we do? Do you believe what you say? That this is a good match?"

She nodded slowly. "I do. He was courteous. He has a good name. And intelligence. Not all have been blessed in such a way."

"Intelligence means shrewdness, cunning," Thales said,

countering her. "He is double my age and then some. What interest could a man of that age find in a thirteen-year-old girl?"

His wife's silence provided all the answers he feared.

Around them, cicadas and song thrushes filled the silence until, finally releasing the air she held in her lungs, Aretaphila sighed.

"This may not be the punishment you believe it to be, Thales. Many are lucky. I was lucky. My kin were lucky. You cannot hold back all our girls because of your sister's fate."

"I do not. Only Medusa." Rubbing the bridge of his nose, Thales groaned. "Oh, to be burdened with daughters," he said. "I would have drowned them at birth had I known the torment it would cause me."

Aretaphila twisted sharply.

"You would not," she said tersely.

Thales laughed sadly. "Of course I would not. I could not have sent her to a riverbed then, any more than I can send her to the wolves now. That is my folly. You say you were lucky in this marriage? A better husband would not be tormented by such trivial a matter."

Aretaphila rested her hand upon her husband's arm.

"This is not a trivial matter, and your concern shows your heart. But they are not all wolves, Thales. They are not all wolves."

Thales moved toward the road, where the wind had already erased the hoofprints in the sand.

"You are wrong, my love. I wish it were not so, but you are. They lick their lips when they see her. These are not men. They are snakes, serpents trying to find the freshest eggs. And when they do find them, they crack them open, devour their insides, and leave nothing more than hollow shells. I feel it in my bones. In every breath. Every time my eyes fall upon her. Myrtis was a full year older than Medusa, with only half her beauty. My sister's fate will not become my daughter's."

"Then what, Thales? What would you have us do?"

———

The journey was long, four days on foot and with little rain to combat the sweltering heat and even less shade to protect them from the searing sun. They traveled alone, the pair of them, and although money was not scarce, they slept under a blanket of only trees and stars. For the first day, despite her father's attempts at conversation, Medusa did not speak, for her heart was raw. Broken by the farewell to her sisters.

"But you will come back soon, won't you?" Stheno, the younger of her two siblings, had clung to her legs. "Because my cartwheeling will be even better then. You will have to watch me. You will come back and watch me, won't you?" Medusa fought back the tears that blurred her sight.

"You still have me." Euryale, the middle child, consoled her younger sister, saving Medusa the discomfort of choking on her words. "I will watch your cartwheeling."

"But you are not as good as Medusa," Stheno protested.

"No," Euryale agreed. "But I am still better than you." She ruffled Stheno's hair until laughter broke in the air.

"Thank you," Medusa whispered.

For the entirety of her life, the seven years between Euryale and Medusa had felt like a full generation and more. The childish ways of her sister—squealing at mice, storming off in tantrums—had led Medusa to believe she would be happier with a full village between them. So many times, Medusa recalled, she had cut their exchanges short, bored by the juvenile content, or else stayed but grown impatient as she considered the more worthwhile ways she could have been spending her time. Now, how she longed to have all those moments back. All the minutes that she had cast her sister aside to water plants or help in the kitchen or simply be by herself and away from the loquaciousness of her younger sibling. *How much would they amount to?* she wondered. All those minutes. A few hours? She knew in an instant that the estimate was too low. A day then perhaps. A week even. A full extra week she could have spent with her sister.

"You never know." Euryale had taken Medusa's hand and clasped it in her own. "Maybe the Goddess will wish for us to come and join you too. Maybe the three of us will be there together in her temple one day."

"Maybe."

"Or perhaps, she will think you are too beautiful to stay there and send you back to us with the riches of a king."

"I am not sure she would send me back *and* give me wealth."

"We shall see," Euryale said, and she embraced her sister.

As Medusa continued to walk beside her father, she tried to recall in her mind every one of those discarded memories. "Forgive me, sister," she whispered to the wind as she walked. "Forgive me."

TWO

FROM THE OUTSIDE, THE TEMPLE APPEARED EMPTY. THE PILLARS, wider than trunks of oak trees and twice as tall, cast shadows on the marble steps, while the subtle scents of rosemary and honeysuckle eddied in the breeze.

"I will wait here for you," Thales said, planting his bag down on the earth before taking a seat beside it.

"You will not come in with me?"

"I cannot, my child. No man may enter the temple of Athena. But I will wait for you here to learn your fate."

Medusa ascended the steps to the temple.

Inside was cavernous. Hundreds of candles lit the walls. Shuddering, Medusa made her way toward them.

"You do not shake in fear, I hope?" said a voice from within the shadows. A woman's voice.

Medusa stopped walking. "Perhaps just a little."

The woman's laughter echoed in the chamber, sonorous and resonant, like the ringing of a crystal glass. "Hopefully, we shall soon put that to rest."

It was as though she created the light. For when she stepped out of the shadows, the shadows themselves disappeared.

"My Goddess." Medusa fell to her knees, the hard clash with the stone stinging her skin. "Forgive me."

Athena shook her head. Her eyes were reminiscent of the polished marble, a glittering gray, contemplative. Hundreds of thousands of thoughts swirled behind them. The pale skin of her bare arms glinted, as did the dagger sheathed at her side.

"There is nothing to forgive." She offered a hand to Medusa. "Please, stand."

Keeping her head bent, Medusa raised herself upward, swallowing back the fear that threatened to consume her. Despite this fear that caused her knees to tremble, she was desperate to glimpse the power that stood before her. The presence of a goddess; it was every mortal's dream.

As if knowing this desire, Athena cupped Medusa's chin with her hand and tilted it up to the sky. Her touch was like water from the sea, a freshness against Medusa's skin, yearned for yet capricious. A cold chill ran down the length of Medusa's spine. The flesh that pressed against her was, she knew, no more similar to her own than dust was to fire. Athena's grip was firm as she twisted the young girl's head from left to right and back again. Through it all, Medusa remained passive and compliant. She had been through this routine countless times since she turned eight, and the frequency of such events had increased with every year. Some men brought bribes disguised as gifts before offering their hand in marriage. Some brought lies disguised as promises or an agreement that their brothers would marry Medusa's sisters when they came of age, "despite their lesser looks." Others would snort and scoff and try to make out that what they saw was nothing special, mundane even, but it was an act, for they all had eyes, and what they saw may well have been carved by the hand of a god.

Medusa let the Goddess inspect her, her gray eyes focused and unmoving throughout the scrutiny. Always the same pressure against her skin, strong and firm. When Athena dropped her hand and stepped back, there was no look of satisfaction or dissatisfaction on her face. Only acceptance.

"Tell me, child." Her right hand rested against her dagger. "What do you think of your father bringing you here to me? To a goddess? Does he think I am an orphanage? A place for children to scrounge and squeal and fill their bellies as they crawl over my floors?" Her voice lilted with mockery. "Or does he think of me as a refuge, perhaps, for all the poor and lazy who fail to lift a scythe to feed their own families? Or I am simply here for all the women who fear the stirring of men? That is why you are here, is it not? Is this what I should expect, prudes and peasants and vermin desecrating my temple?"

Medusa made no movement as she spoke.

"I am not here to desecrate anything, my Goddess."

"Then what? Why are you here? You want to offer yourself?" She laughed. The heat of her immortality radiated only inches from Medusa's face. The comparative ease of only moments ago had been replaced with a bitter, harsher timbre that hummed in the air like the static of thunder before a storm. "Offer yourself to the men of Athens, Medusa. They will pay a richer sum than I will. Your face, your youth, you could name your price." She combed her fingers through a ringlet of Medusa's hair. "Does that not tempt you? Imagine the life you could buy. The life your sisters would have. Surely you would be a fool not to consider it." Athena's gaze narrowed.

"Why do you not defend yourself, child? Speak. Give me

your reasoning. Perhaps that was not your father I saw outside the temple. Perhaps you are the bastard child that haunts his nightmares." Her lips twisted wryly. "Or perhaps you do not haunt his nightmares at all. Perhaps he needed you away, the temptation of those perfect curls and sprouting breasts too great. Perhaps the trip here was the chance he longed for. The chance to have you to himself. After all, you had money. You could have stayed in the best inns on your journey here, but instead, you chose the moon as your blanket. Why did your father wish to keep you to himself, child? Perhaps the suitors who came calling would be disappointed in the purity they received?"

Medusa's pulse surged, although she locked her jaw, refusing to rise to the Goddess's bait. She could not hold her tongue forever; she knew that. The Goddess was not known for her patience, and it would not take long before her silence was viewed as insolence. But she would not have words forced from her through invectives. The starkness of the silence was subdued by a single birdsong, one stray halcyon that seemed to not appreciate the weight of the moment.

"Speak, child." Athena's slender fingers had returned to combing Medusa's hair. Her tone once more softened, her eyes welcoming. "I wish to hear your words. I have heard such things about that voice of yours. And you have traveled so far to get here. So very, very far."

For the first time since entering the temple, Medusa felt the weight of her journey and the true gravity of the task ahead of her. The blisters and sores smarted on the soles of her feet.

"We can sit if you wish." Athena noticed the wavering of her eyes. "You must be tired."

"You are a goddess," Medusa said, ignoring the Goddess's suggestion. "You know there were no inns, so you know there were no misdoings. And you know the reason for me being here."

Athena pressed the tips of her fingers together. The luminous glow of her skin glistened.

"So, a refuge? That is right, is it not? Your father wished me to take on his burdens. Clothe you, feed you, and allow you to siphon off my prosperity. Why do you stay silent?" The slant of her eyebrows rose up toward the crease in her skin where her helmet so often would lie. "You are right; I have watched you, child. I have seen that tongue of yours cut men twice your size to ribbons. I have seen you sell your father's grapes for double their worth to men you knew could afford it, only to give away your profits to others with no worth. You have words, child, a library's worth of words. Why do you choose not to use them?"

Medusa's gaze held firm. Respectful, but firm.

"Because, my Goddess, you have seen me. You know what my tongue can do. What my hand can make and weave and bake. You have seen my heart, my will, and my father's and mother's and sisters' too. What words I speak or do not, now, at this moment, will have no bearing on what happens to me. You are a goddess. Had you wished to, you could have overturned our journey a dozen times or more. You did not. A word, a dozen words now. I do not believe that a goddess would strip or salvage a person based on one action when they have a thousand behind them and a hundred thousand yet to come. Your decision was made before I stepped foot into this temple. All that awaits me is to hear it."

Athena stepped back. On her belt, the dagger glinted, brighter than before. A sliver of green flashed about her ankles as an embroidered serpent looped around the hem of her robe. The knocking in Medusa's chest quickened as the gray-eyed goddess narrowed her gaze, once again sharpening her features and voice.

"And you think I have chosen to take you in?" Her tone was

derisive. "Of all the girls who appear to me, who line up, their arms laden with gifts, and you believe I will take *you*?"

"I do not know that," Medusa said, with a calm rationality of one much older. "For all I know, you may strike me down and kick me to the cobbles of Athens before the night has fallen. If that is the case, then so be it. I know I cannot change the mind of the mighty Athena. And I know it would be foolish of me even to try."

Athena walked a path around the girl, another procession that Medusa had been subjected to before. She kept her head forward, her shoulders back.

"So you have wisdom?" Athena said.

"For a child," Medusa replied.

The hint of a smile flickered on Athena's lips.

"Wisdom is only part of me. Part of my temple. What of the war? What do you know of that?" She stopped her circling. "You have never stood upon a battlefield. You have never held the warm spillage of a man's belly as his breath fades from his lungs. Your senses have never been filled with the stench of blood while those around you swing swords and scream for your death. What good would you be to me? You are a child. You are soft and weak."

The child's tongue drew a circle across her lips, pink and vibrant against her skin. Her eyes glided upward, not so far as to meet the Goddess's, but close enough.

"It is true," Medusa said, her child's voice slow and contemplative. "I have not stood on a battlefield. I am no daughter of Sparta, born with the weight of a sword and the knowledge of a swing already coursing through me. I do not know wars, but I know of battles. Battles waged in my family's name when my first suitor came calling when I was just eight. Battles I waged when I refused to let men's hands wander where they felt they had a right to, or when I refused to follow them on a walk, down a path, or into an olive grove. I know of the battles I have waged as I stood in a marketplace and demanded that men look not at my breasts or my eyes or my legs, but at the fruit which I was selling. These were not battles of blood, it is true, but they are battles. Battles that I have fought and won."

Athena stepped back from the girl. Her light had diffused, now softened and muted.

"And these wars you have waged," she said, running her hand against her dagger. "You think these will end once you enter my temple? Once you are a priestess of mine?"

For the first time since leaving her family home, it was Medusa's turn to smile. Her lips turned upward, the smile rising to her cheeks. But the glimmer that came from her eyes was not one of joy. It was dark and hollow and not earned in her lifetime but in all the thousands of lifetimes that had gone before her. By her aunt, by her aunt's aunt, and by generations too far back to recall.

"Those battles," she said. "They don't ever end."

THREE

HELIOS WAS LAYING CLAIM TO THE SKY WITH A SMALL SMUDGE of purple creasing the horizon. Medusa had risen while there were more stars still and had been sweeping the temple since she dressed. She was to meet with members of the polis that day. She was to stand before these men and women on Athena's behalf, answer their questions, and bestow the Goddess's wisdom as best she knew how. This was the third time in as many moons that this responsibility had fallen to her. In the outside world, other women may have been made jealous of this, seen it as favoritism by the Goddess, but in the temple such thoughts were kept to themselves. There was nothing to be gained from belittling another; their tables would always be laid with the same food, their beds still covered in the same linen.

Her hands gripped the broom as she swept the temple floor, sending motes of dust spiraling upward and adding a thousand extra stars to the morning's dimming constellations. When her footsteps no longer showed imprints on the ground, she picked up her tools and headed downstairs to the chamber beneath the temple. There she cleaned her hands and feet, scrubbed them with sage and oranges, and draped her tunic across her body. She twisted the headband of the Priestess around her forehead and draped the white shawl over her shoulders. Some in her position wore gold and jewelry to such an occasion, but her aim was never to blind a man's eyes, merely to enter into them.

"He is stealing," the man said to her. "Again and again. Three times this week, stealing from me. This is my family's food. Their money, their gold."

"He has stolen gold as well as food?" Medusa asked.

"What buys the food if not the gold?"

"Your wife on her back, from what I hear," someone shouted from the crowd. The man's face flashed with anger before he turned back to the Priestess.

Medusa was sitting upon a wooden stool, while a pool of men puddled around her, waiting to have their grievances heard. Rosemary and lemon balm burned on the ground, their heady aromas thickening the air surrounding her.

"Have you offered him food?" Medusa's response traveled clearly to the man, although he shook his head as if her words did not make sense.

"He is stealing from me. Why would I give him food?"

"Because he is stealing from you. Offer him food. No man wants what can be given to him freely. Your fruits taste no sweeter than another's. Offer your food to him. I would be surprised if he continued to steal."

"What if he refuses to take the food?" the man questioned, his cheeks still pink with annoyance.

"Then perhaps he will have realized the error in his actions through your compassion. If he accepts it and the stealing continues, perhaps a blind eye could be cast."

The tightening of the man's jaw indicated distinct disapproval.

"So, I am just to let him steal?" he said.

Medusa sat back on her stool and surveyed the man. His chin was dimpled, and his dark hair slick to his scalp. Around his arm wove a gold band, wider than his wrist. "Sir, would you give your food to the gods if they so asked for it?"

The man shook his head in bemusement. "Of course. Any sane man would."

"And if a god were to steal?"

"The gods can take and give as they please."

Medusa smiled. "They can," she said. "So we are in agreement. But"—she paused and shifted back a little—"what if this god is disguised? Such as Poseidon when he comes to the shore. How could you tell whether the man you are refusing food to is a mortal or a god?"

The quiver of the man's chin continued. "This neighbor has lived beside me all my life."

"And yet you only ever see him when your eyes are open. Where, I pray, does he go when they are closed or your head is turned?"

The man blushed. His questioning had lasted longer than it needed to, and behind him came the grousing of those who still required the Priestess's audience.

"You asked for the wisdom of the Goddess, and that is what you have been bestowed," she said to the man. "Do you understand me?"

With a locked jaw, the man bowed his head and nodded in quick succession.

"Thank you, my lady," he said, shuffling back into the crowd.

Most of the queries that came her way that day were silly

quibbles and reconcilable differences. Men stealing food, men stealing women, men stealing livestock, livestock that men often thought
of more fondly than they did their women. Men didn't need gods,
Medusa mused; they just needed somebody, anybody, to guide them
in their lives.

"My daughter has been sent home in disgrace," a man said,
stepping in front of the crowd and stealing Medusa's attention. "This
husband was her second. The dowry nearly cost me my livelihood.
Why must she do this? Why must she burden herself, disgrace herself
in this manner? Can she not see she will soon be too old to marry,
and we will have no money for a suitable match?"

"Is your daughter here?" Medusa asked.

The man shook his head. "This is not a place for women," he
replied. Medusa raised an eyebrow.

"Tell me, how has your daughter disgraced you? What acts have
burdened your soul so heavily?"

The man's brow crinkled.

"No man will marry her now," he said. "She will be forced to stay
at home and tend crops until the day she dies."

"And does she know this?"

"How could she not?"

Medusa's hand rose to her forehead, where a thin curl had slipped
from beneath her headband. The man reminded her of her father,
with so many worries etched into his forehead. He could be the same
age too, she thought, for it had been over five years since she had bid
him farewell on the steps to Athena's temple.

"Sir, you are a good man," she said. "Better, possibly, than the
hundred men who have spoken before you today. You have stood
and told me only of your daughter's disgrace, of the burden upon
herself that she has caused."

The man nodded solemnly.

"But these are your daughter's disgraces to choose. You speak of her burdens now, but did you ask of her burdens before?" The man remained silent as he chewed on his thumbnail. "It is not a life you would have chosen for her; I understand that. One of toil and uncertainty. But what is a burden for some is freedom for another. A snake charmer earns his living where others would find their demise. A sailor spends years at sea, when others may perish in a week. You have raised her well. Trust her."

The evening in Athens was muggy and damp. Bodies bustled in the alleyways, shouting and laughing, fighting and embracing. The sky was colored with an orange hue and the warm air above the buildings, blurring the birds as they flitted from rooftop to rooftop. When she reached the temple, Medusa bowed her head to the statue of her goddess before climbing the steps.

"Medusa?" The name came from a shadow, a dark corner by the edge of the steps. "Can you help me?"

A woman appeared, folded over and crumpled to half her height, holding her hands out to the Priestess. Her body was draped in a brown shawl, thick and harsh like the sack of a beggar. Her hair was matted, dark brown-red, and her head bowed, perfect circles of red dropping to the ground by her feet.

"Cornelia?" Medusa said, her eyes scanning the sea of faces that swam in front of the temple. "Quickly, quickly. Get inside. You should not have waited out here."

She wrapped her arms around the figure and ushered her inside the temple walls, her eyes still moving from side to side.

"Does he know where you are? Did he follow you?"

The woman shook her head. "No, no. I do not think so. I came on foot. No one will have recognized me. I told no one in the house."

"You came by foot all this way?" Medusa felt a heavy ache in her chest. She could only imagine the trail of blood that had been left on the stones. She reached a hand down to the woman's shoulder.

"Show me," she said.

Cornelia's breath was labored as she slipped the brown shawl down around her waist. A small gasp erupted from behind them. Medusa spun around, stifling the shock of the other priestess with a wave of her hand.

Beneath the beggar garments, Cornelia wore robes of silk, stained with brown and red. Around her wrists were bracelets and bangles, not only of gold and silver but also of black and purple that were still growing. The marks around her neck and arms mimicked so clearly the handprints made by a child in the mud, thumbs and fingers and nails having carved out divots in her young flesh.

"What happened?" Medusa asked, taking a bowl handed to her by another priestess.

"I found him with… I found him." She stopped herself, needing no further explanation. "I did not mean to, I swear." Her voice quivered. "I was not spying. I was not snooping. I merely entered the chamber and…and…" Her trembling shook loose the tears brimming in her eyes.

As gently as a butterfly on a petal, Medusa laid a cloth around the woman's wrist and began wiping away the blood.

"I believe he wished me dead," she said. "I fear that may be true," Medusa agreed.

This meeting was not their first. Medusa had been present at the wedding of the girl some four years prior as an indication of Athena's approval of the pairing. Given that the child was the same age as Medusa had been when the suitors came calling, it was impossible not to feel a bond. The betrothed was a military leader, an honorable man and, as such, had been seen as an extremely favorable arrangement. That day had been filled with wine, so much so that few were standing by the time Medusa had left. Laughter and music carried from the wedding as she draped her evening shawl around her shoulders and headed back to the temple. But the joy did not touch Medusa. For when, during the blessing, the young woman's eyes had looked at Medusa, they conveyed only fear. Fear of the unknown. Fear of the known, but not yet experienced. Fear, possibly of the experiences so far. It was not an unusual response, Medusa knew. Most women looked fearful on the wedding night, and those who didn't generally showed no emotion at all.

But months passed, and the look did not fade. The child, when Medusa saw her, would recoil into the shadow of her husband. Even when her belly grew big with child, she did not beam and grin the way so many did when they were to bear their first or any offspring. And when the child arrived, it was as though her will detached from her body altogether. Over the past two years, she had often arrived with bruised cheeks and blue ribs, although none so dark as these.

"Is there not somewhere you can go?" Medusa asked, rinsing the red cloth in the bowl and wringing out the bloody water with her hands. "Is there not a brother, an uncle?"

Cornelia shook her head. "No. Maybe. Perhaps."

"You have family?"

Her brow creased before she gave a single nod.

"I have a cousin. On the island of Cephalonia. But what would I do there?" she said. "I have no training. No skills. My husband would find me."

"You do not know that. You are young. There is time for you to learn."

"So, when he finds me, he will kill a skilled woman? And my daughter, what sort of life would she have by growing up on the rocks of an island?" She shook her head, the action causing a spasm of pain to twist upon her mouth. "It is better I come here," she said. "To the temple of the Goddess. No husband can beat a woman for coming to a temple, can he?" She spoke with the smallest of laughs, although her eyes continued to betray her fear.

"We will get you clean and find a place for you," Medusa said. "I will find you a place."

Medusa lifted her hand to guide the woman to the chambers behind the temple, but she did not move.

"Cornelia?"

The young woman's eyes fell to the marble floor. Her toes pressed together.

"There is something else," she said.

A chill ran the length of Medusa's spine, and she muttered a prayer to Athena. The sounds of caterwauling from the city streets masked the silence as the Priestess waited. She knew what would come next. Slowly, Cornelia unwrapped the shawl from around her hips. The bloodstain reached her knees.

"I was with child," she said. "I was with another child. But I fear it has gone. My child has gone, hasn't it?"

Medusa stayed silent, for she knew there were no words that could stem such a pain.

Once the wounds were washed and wrapped, they dressed the woman in the garb of the priestesses. The bleeding had not stopped and would not for many days, an older priestess had told her. But should the pains persist past the next moon, she was to return and bathe in the fountains of the Goddess. She was fortunate it was early, the older priestess had said as she pinched the color to Cornelia's cheeks. It was better when it was early. Medusa had difficulty seeing how any aspect of the situation could be considered fortunate.

"These silks are almost as fine as mine," Cornelia said, attempting joviality as she pulled the sleeves of the robe over her welted skin. "Perhaps I should have joined the Goddess rather than marry."

"You can still find another way. I will write to your cousin. As soon as we hear any news, we will send for you. For now, we will find you a place to sleep tonight." Medusa took the girl's hand, but her gesture was met with silence. Cornelia's eyes, which for so long had looked pleadingly to Medusa, now refused even to meet hers.

"Medusa. I thank you. You have tended me well."

"Cornelia…"

"It is late. There are only so many hours for which a woman can pray and have her husband not feel abandoned."

Medusa reached to touch her shoulder, but remembering the bruises, she withdrew.

"Cornelia, no. You do not need to return to him."

"Yes, I do."

"No, you don't."

"You would turn me into an islander. A farmworker." Her pretty face contorted. "You would have me digging in the dirt and sharing a mattress of straw with the rats and the vermin? How could I live such a life?"

"You would live it. You would be alive. You do not need to return to him."

"Yes, I do."

"No, you—"

"Yes. My wife is correct. She needs to return home now."

He stood in the light of the entrance, his bronzed arms out, his bare knuckles worn red and bloody from the resilience of his wife's flesh. There was a nervousness to his stance, an edge to his eye.

Fury, almost unearthly in its intensity, swarmed Medusa. She stepped toward him.

"This is the temple of the Goddess." The wrath in her voice made the air tremble. "You are not permitted here."

The snake eyes of the man smiled upward as if she had done no more than ask him the price of a fig.

"I do not wish to intrude. I have merely come to retrieve what is mine. Are your prayers done, my love?" He spoke past Medusa to his wife, who shook behind her. "I know the gods will have listened to you. I am certain. And what timing have I that I appear at the moment you wish? It is as though we were cut from one cloth."

Cornelia's feet remained rooted to the ground. The bravado with which she previously had spoken evaporated into the air.

"Cornelia." Her husband's tone grew harsher.

"Sir," Medusa spoke again. "This is the temple of Athena. Leave here."

"I will leave when I have what I came for."

"You should leave now, with what little of your dignity remains." Anger flashed in his eyes.

"You would question me?" He stepped forward into the temple. Medusa gasped as if his foot had buried itself into her stomach rather than simply crossed the threshold of the temple. His fingers flexed. Her eyes blazed.

"You wish to strike down a priestess in the temple of the Goddess of War?" Medusa asked.

"I do not wish to," he replied.

"Then leave."

The man shook his head.

"I will leave when I get what I came for."

"You will. The gods will see you here. They will see you, here, this day; mark my words. You know no wrath like that of a goddess whose temple has been defiled."

She stood her ground, hands quivering against her hips, no fear, only fury.

"I do not wish to harm you, Priestess. I have only come for what is mine."

"You have no claim on her in here. And you will not defile the name of Athena," Medusa repeated.

From behind her, Cornelia's stuttering breaths echoed. "I am coming. I am coming with you, my love."

Medusa spun around, breathless.

"You cannot."

"Look at you two, bickering over a silly mistake." She laughed, high and false. Her eyes glanced across Medusa as her feet skipped over the ground. Both landed beside her husband. She took his hand and swept her arms around him, grimacing in pain as she did so. Medusa's eyes were drawn to her belly. A belly where, only hours ago, a small heart had trembled, so tiny that only the gods could have heard. Cornelia turned toward the entrance.

Only at the point of departure did she glance back toward Medusa. She mouthed something, perhaps a word of endearment, perhaps an apology. Which, Medusa would never know.

FOUR

THREE DAYS LATER, A SLAVE CAME TO THE TEMPLE. THE MAN WAS young, his dark skin marked with pink stripes. He walked with his head down and waited at the steps of the temple. When another priestess approached him, he asked for Medusa by name.

"My master says he has no more need for this." The messenger pressed an item into the palm of Medusa's hand. The gold of the ring was dull and tarnished, a crust of red muting the shine.

"And your mistress?" The words tumbled from Medusa's mouth, her tongue and throat numb.

"An accident." The man's eyes scuttled across the ground.

Weeping was not her custom, not anymore. She had cried that first night when her father left her. The Goddess had gone too and she was alone, not just in the temple but indeed the world. In the privacy of a quiet corner, she had allowed herself a moment.

There had been other times in the early days. The sight of a bloodied child or a baby, still from birth, had caused tears to rise up and fall freely. Most of the time they went unnoticed, drowned out by the mother's own wails and cries. Gradually, over the years, her heart had hardened to such matters. It was life. Children were beaten, babies died, and every year, countless women were lost in the same way as Cornelia. Some of them had come to the temple seeking the strength to pull away. Few had had the courage to see it through. Some stayed with their husbands for the children; some for the gold. Many because they held fast to a hope, no matter how ill-founded, that their husbands might change.

And so, Medusa had become accustomed to the way these events would play out, and every one caused the rock in her chest to harden further. But for Cornelia, the tears refused to be abated.

"You take this one too hard, child," Athena said as Medusa wept into her wine. She had left her duties at the polis and laid herself to bed in the chambers beneath the temple. It had taken some hours before the tears had given way to sleep, and even when it came, it was shallow and short. When she awoke, there was a shimmer to the air, and the Goddess was by her side.

"She chose to return to this man," Athena said, caressing her hair like she was a child. "That is on her head. You cannot blame yourself."

"I do not," Medusa said. "I blame him. For every last drop of her blood."

"Good."

"But he will not pay for it."

"He will. The gods will see that he does."

Medusa snorted.

"You do not believe me?" Athena's hand stopped.

"The gods are the ones that cause this," Medusa answered. "Their power, their strength. Their stubborn anger and terror. They show man everything they cannot have control over and, as such, force men to claim dominion over the one thing that they can."

"So, you blame me? You think I have a role in this?"

Medusa shifted up from where she lay.

"You, my Goddess, no. Never." She sighed deeply. "Why is it that women are viewed as unstable? Women hold knives more often in the day than men ever do, yet it is not women who stab their husbands to death when they fear adultery. Women gather in clusters with friendships stronger than steel, yet it is not women who beat their husbands to the ground in gangs when a hint of wrongdoing echoes in the air. It is not women who require lover after lover, then make promises of love that they recant when darker hair and deeper eyes are cast in their direction. Time and time again, we are called out as the emotional ones, the irrational ones. Women don't get drunk like men and hurl insults at strangers or throw rocks in protests. Women use words and reason where men use fists and force. So why are we always second? Why is that, my Goddess? Why are we always second?"

Medusa waited, a longing in her heart to hear the wise words of her idol, but for once, the Goddess of Wisdom had little she could respond with. "Sometimes, the lines are blurred, Medusa." Athena rose up to standing. "Sometimes, it is difficult to see where your feet are planted when you are focusing so far out to the horizon. But we will not talk of this in here, in my place of peace. I will come to you again soon." She bowed and kissed Medusa on her head, and Medusa's skin prickled as if ice and sunlight had been poured there.

Taking leave from her duties, Medusa stood at the side and watched as Cornelia's husband took a torch and brought it to his wife's pyre. The day was cold. A chilled breeze whipped up from the sea, spraying the air with crystals of salt and causing the flames to spit and sizzle as they licked around the corpse. He had little need of robes for warmth, Medusa thought, watching as false tears slid down his cheeks. Bowing his head, he accepted embraces from every lady who offered. As the sun slipped below the horizon, Medusa stayed, hovering in the distance, listening to the condolences that he drank with as much ease as the wine that filled his goblet. Wine served by girls whose flesh he pinched, more like a farmer inspecting the quality of his cattle than a husband mourning his wife. It was not uncommon, of course; he would hardly be the first person to numb his grief through drink. Only, from what she had seen, there was no grief, not real grief. As the day passed into night, Medusa continued to watch. She herself abstained from the wine; the sweetness would be soured by the bile of her wrath, which grew with every passing moment. She watched as his hand slid effortlessly into that of another woman, and then from her hand to her thigh and higher still. She watched as laughter rocked his belly and he raised toasts, not to his wife but to his good fortune in life.

When she could watch no longer, Medusa grasped the closest goblet to her, poured the wine down her throat, and marched to meet him.

"Your wife has only just left this world," she spat. "You think this shows decency?"

"Priestess?" he slurred, a sneer corkscrewing his features. "Come, join us." He patted the embroidered throw, which draped the seat beside him. "There is plenty more room here."

Medusa spat on the ground.

"You are nothing more than a murderer," she said.

The man scoffed.

"I am plenty more, and, I believe, I can show you such. Come, take another wine."

Medusa hesitated, then took the goblet from his hand. A moment later, a wave of red sprayed into the air.

Mortal guests at the funeral were not the only ones who saw the wine fly through the air that evening. Dressed in the garb of a lord, Poseidon watched with glee as the priestess threw her words and wine without inhibition.

He turned to the man next to him and asked, "This woman, who is she?"

"She is the priestess, Medusa, from the temple of Athena."

Poseidon smiled to himself. "She has fire."

FIVE

THE FIRST TIME HE CAME TO SEE HER, HE WAITED ON THE steps of the temple. For two weeks, he had watched her, studied her, his mind on nothing else. Out on the islands, he let storms rage and ships be dashed against the rocks, for they did not matter now. Poseidon had other thoughts at play. Beautiful, devious thoughts. The first week he had come as a merchant—wealthy, handsome, alluring. It was a disguise he had picked for many such occasions. He carried a flask full of wine and a purse of gems that he tipped onto his hand and demanded extravagant prices for. Women and men flocked around him, eyes wide at the sight.

But while others were enthralled by his exotic tales and charming quips, Medusa paid him no heed and walked past the god and his wares every day, without a second glance. If anything, his jewels appeared to repulse her.

It did not take long for Poseidon to realize the Priestess had no time to wander aimlessly, listening to merchants spin tales. And so, he reconsidered his approach. Different fish needed different hooks.

He picked the time of day when he knew she would be returning from the polis. He had been there himself, this time disguised as an old man, seeking out her wisdom on how best to deal with a troublesome mare. Her answer had been thoughtful, although he watched only the movement of her lips and cared not for the words that left them.

"Excuse me, Priestess," he said, speaking as Medusa ascended the steps. His new guise was a great deal younger than the one from earlier in the day. "Excuse me." Medusa turned to face him. Her hair was covered in a shawl, and the fine dust from the day had turned the white of the silk to a subtle, glinting amber. Her headband had slipped ever so slightly to one side, allowing her ringlets to break free and drop down about her shoulders.

"I have an offering for the Goddess," he said, holding out a platter and casting his eye toward the temple. "I was hoping I could deliver it." He had picked his outfit carefully for the occasion. Too flamboyant and she would dismiss him instantly, the way she had the merchant. Too poor and she would be circumspect as to how he had come by such an offering in the first place.

"Thank you," Medusa said. She reached out her hand and took hold of the silver platter laden with delicacies. His fingers held firmly on to the other side.

"Would it be possible for me to take it myself?" he asked. "Into the temple?"

"It would not," Medusa said. "No men are allowed in the temple of Athena."

The man nodded thoughtfully. "Even with you by my side?"

"No men are permitted in the temple," Medusa repeated. She spoke forcefully, but kindly. Poseidon continued his nodding. His grip remained firm around the platter.

"It is my wife, you see," he said, offering the Priestess the most pleading look he could muster. "I wish to thank Athena for my wife."

"Is your wife not well, sir?" Medusa asked. "Can she not come to the temple herself?"

The man smiled. It was a great smile, he knew, yet it was not reciprocated in quite the manner he had hoped.

"She is quite well, thank you, Priestess," he said. "But that is why I wish to give thanks to your goddess. She was ill, and I feared the worst, but my wife prayed to Athena and only Athena every day and every night, and on the fifth day, the fever receded. My wife will come to make an offering when she is fully recovered," he said. "But I wanted to give one myself. To display my gratitude."

"That is thoughtful," Medusa said. "And the Goddess will look favorably upon this act. I will ensure she receives this offering." He smiled again to the best of his mortal marionette's ability.

"But I cannot go to her myself?"

"You cannot," Medusa said.

Reluctantly, he dropped his hands from the platter and bowed his head.

"Thank you," he said.

The next day, he waited again outside the temple. The offering was smaller this time, not nearly so lavish—for how would it look if he were to offer a greater gift now? Like his first offering had been miserly. Like he had misled her about their means. Medusa would spot that flaw without a doubt. Once again he picked a place at the bottom of the steps, and this time when he called her it was not by her title, but by her name.

"Medusa," he said. The Priestess stopped. She lifted her head and turned. "I am sorry if I speak out of turn. I told my wife of our encounter yesterday, and she assured me that it must have been the priestess Medusa to whom I spoke."

"Your wife was correct. Though I do not believe you told me her name?"

A slight rise in tension flickered across the god's smile.

"Caroline," he said, which was a familiar name among the ladies of Athens. "I cannot rest," he said. "We are hosting her family today and did not wish to seem rude, but she asked me to offer you these. They are for you," he emphasized.

"That is most kind, sir."

"Really, it is nothing. Think of it as an apology for my previous intrusion."

With his sentence floating in the air, he turned and placed his hand upon hers. Her warmth flowed into him like a fine wine. Then, in an instant, he twisted and strode down the steps. Medusa's eyes were still on him, his sudden departure clearly leaving her intrigued. The heat of her hand was still fresh on his fingertips. It was exactly as he wished.

SIX

THE DAY HE ENTERED THE TEMPLE, THE HEAT WAS SO STIFLING that the birds, which normally skimmed and dipped around the roof, had rested their feathers down on the marble floor in an attempt to siphon some of the heat away from their bodies. The worshippers had left, their offerings taken and blessings given upon them in the name of the gray-eyed goddess. Around the walls and before the altars, two dozen candles burned to the end of their wicks, the white wax dripping and pooling around the holders. The other priestesses had been called away. He had seen to it. A child with a fever, a distraught wife, any incident that required the aid of a priestess. It had been no small task, even for a god, to ensure that no stone was left unturned, no other priestess left in attendance. Most of the women had been asked for by name so that even when Medusa offered to go instead, they told her she must stay behind. They could manage, they said. If not, they would send for her.

And manage they could. For when the priestesses arrived at their destinations, some having traveled miles on foot, they were surprised to find that the children were not so sick as they had been led to believe, nor the wives so woeful. Still, they stayed a while and drank and ate with the families, for they had walked far, and it would be an equally long journey back to the temple.

Medusa knelt in front of the candles. Tonight, her thoughts lingered on her family. She had heard rumor after rumor of them since her departure. A mixture of tales that may or may not have whispers of the truth to them. Recently, the rumors had been that one of her sisters had married. It seemed unfeasible. After all, the eldest, Euryale, was just thirteen. While many parents would have seen their daughters sold at such an age, it seemed unlikely of hers. Unless, of course, they had fallen upon hard times. But rumors changed like the wind, a slight embellishment or omission from each tongue that tells the story, twisting and distorting the tale further and further. Besides, a more favorable one may well make its way to her by the time the week was out.

Lost in her thoughts, Medusa was gazing at the candles when something broke her reverie. There were no footsteps or voices, just the rustling of feathers and the beating of wings as the birds abandoned their place in the cool and flew upward into the warm air that they had previously sought sanctuary from. Out of the corner of her eye, Medusa saw the shadow. A figure swallowed by the darkness.

"Can I help you?" she said, standing up and turning. "Do you seek help from the Goddess?"

"From Athena? No." The man's voice caused chills to spread across Medusa's arms and down to the base of her spine. "For all her glory, she cannot satisfy me."

"Sir," she said. The deep voice was unrecognizable to her. "You are not permitted to be here. I must ask you to leave."

"But this is a house of gods," he said. "So, the house belongs more to me than to you. And yet, I do not ask you to leave, Priestess."

The figure stepped into the light. She blinked, confused.

"I know you. You gave gifts to the Goddess."

"I gave gifts to you."

Medusa frowned as her thoughts cleared. "Gifts from your wife. That is right? You gave gifts from your wife. Caroline, is that not her name?"

The laugh that followed was loud and deep and shook the pillars of the earth in a way Medusa had never known.

"My wife? Oh yes, she is somewhere, casting her net, out there with the urchins and the eels."

The hammering of Medusa's pulse grew faster and stronger as she searched for a place of safety in the shadows. "Who are you? Why are you here?"

The man smiled. His eyes glinted with fire and water, together in an unending torrent.

"Which question should I answer first?" he said as he stepped toward her. "Who am I, or why am I here?"

Medusa stepped back, her muscles shaking. She took hold of one of the candles and thrust it out in front of her, pointing the flame toward the man. The melting wax gave way between her fingers, searing her skin, but she did not let go. Not until his body was only feet away from hers, only inches from the flame, did she hurl it with all her might.

The laugh echoed around her.

"Did you expect that to hurt me?" He snorted in her face. "And I thought you were wise, Medusa. What kind of priestess is Athena keeping here if you think that a tiny flame could even mark a god? I fear you have been misled. Perhaps we both have."

Trembling, Medusa stood firm and faced his watery eyes.

"I have misled no one," she said. "This is the temple of Athena, and you are not permitted to enter here."

His face lost any trace of amusement. His eyes darkened.

"I am Poseidon," he said. "And I will enter where I choose."

Her arms and legs were pinned, her voice silenced by his hand, which, tasting of salt and sea, he clasped over her mouth to drown her screams. Even with her eyes screwed shut, tears ran unendingly down her cheeks. How long it lasted, she could not say, for time lost all meaning, stretched and elongated beyond all possibility. At that moment, Medusa naively thought and believed this would be the worst that would befall her in this lifetime. She had no idea how wrong she was.

Even then, for Medusa, worse than her own defilement was the defilement of the temple of the goddess she loved. This place of sanctuary was now desecrated and dishonored. She thought of the women who came to her, of Cornelia, and wondered how many times they had suffered this fate at the hands of their husbands. Her cousins, her aunt, who had died at the hands of such a man. Only this was not a man. This was a god. His pressure against her body reminded her with every passing heartbeat. His body slick as oil, the ichor pumping beneath his skin. Her tears stung, their salt bitter between her lips. Anger surged through her. How dare he come and take what was not his, and in this sacred place. Medusa decided she would look him in the eyes and show him that he might take her flesh, but he would never have dominion over her spirit. Her eyes flickered open. It was then that she saw them.

They had only just stepped into the temple. A mother, her two daughters, and a baby. By their side was another priestess. Their mouths hung open, eyes wide. Medusa tried to cry out to them and, at that moment, realized her mouth was no longer gagged. Her arms no longer pinned but flat by her side, her legs spread open. Poseidon was gone. Too numb to move or speak or cry, she lay on the cold marble, her eyes locked on the mother, and as the woman clutched her infant to her chest, undisguised disgust adorned her face. Medusa's heart fell like a stone statue and shattered into a thousand pieces.

SEVEN

THE FAMILY LEFT, THE PRIESTESS USHERING THEM OUTSIDE.
They said things, shouted things, screamed things at her
as they went. Not that Medusa could hear their words.
Her mind was a fog, and her arms were red and bruised with the
fingerprints she had seen so often on women who came to her. Pain
spasmed through her cells. Pain in places she did not know could
feel pain. Her breaths were shuddering, shallow, and for the briefest
time, she thought that perhaps, if she let them, they would just stop
altogether. If she closed her eyes, her heart would slow, and the air
would escape her, never to return. But the moment did not last.
Girding against the pain, she rolled her body over and pushed herself
onto her knees.

With her head bowed toward the melting candles, anyone who
had entered would have thought she was in prayer, the same way she
had been those long minutes ago when Poseidon entered the temple.
But a twist in time was not something any god would offer. All their
words, all their promises. All she could hope was that her goddess
would avenge her.

After some time, the tears stopped, and the pain drifted back into a dull throb. *Will this be it forever?* she wondered. This hollowness that ached all the way to her bones.

"Tell me it is not true." Medusa jerked around, a sharp pain stabbing her stomach. The Goddess stood before her, dagger in hand. "Tell me what I hear are lies."

Medusa's lungs heaved, her eyes instantly awash with tears. "I am sorry, my Priestess. I am so sorry."

Athena's eyes widened. "So, it is true? You allowed him in here. Into you?"

Medusa pushed herself upward and pressed her palms against the serpents of her goddess's robe.

"Allowed? No, never."

Athena shook her head.

"You were seen, Medusa. You were seen eyes wide, on your back, moaning with pleasure, allowing him to enter you."

Medusa shook her head back in return. The words of the Goddess blurring in her mind.

"He forced me. He tricked me. He told me he was married."

Athena's face wrinkled in disgust.

"You would allow a married man between your legs, in my temple?"

"Please, my Goddess—"

"You would defile my temple because of your lust?"

"No!" Medusa wept. "Please, you do not understand…"

The words had flown from her mouth. She gasped at the air with all the breath she possessed, but she could not draw them back within her. Athena stepped back, swiping Medusa's hands away from her. Her eyes were black with rage.

"I do not understand?"

"Please, my—"

"I, a goddess, the Goddess of Wisdom, *do not understand* what *you*, a mortal, are saying? I understand plenty, my child."

"Please, please…" Medusa groveled on the ground at the Goddess's feet.

"I have seen the eyes men show to you, and I have seen the coyness you return."

"No—"

"I have seen how your words linger, and your gaze is oh so full of compassion." She punctured the air with every word.

"Athena, my—"

"How dare you use my name. I put my faith and trust in you. Took you in when your father wished to protect you from the lustful eyes of men, but maybe it was they who needed protecting from your wanton ways. And how am I repaid? You sully my temple, my sanctuary with your lust."

"I would not… I did not…" Sounds caught and stumbled on her lips as she fought for the words that she knew in her heart were true. She raised herself to her feet. "I did not want his gaze," she said. "I do not want any man's gaze."

A smile curled on Athena's lips, her gray eyes shimmering and cold.

"Well, we shall see if your word is true," she replied.

The Goddess had vanished as quickly as she entered, knocking Medusa to the ground in a blaze of light. Her head smacked against the ridged white marble pillar. *This is my end*, she reflected as a pain burned across her scalp, equal to a thousand tiny needles forcing up through her skin. *Athena's farewell to me has been my death.*

Another priestess approached. Medusa saw her shadow hovering close by, but she did not raise her head. She did not want to see the venom or pity in the woman's eyes any more than she wanted others to see the shame in hers.

"Leave her," someone called. A sigh of relief wafted through Medusa. Her mind drifted back to her family's groves. What she would give to walk beneath those trees one last time and brush her hand against the iridescent leaves of the olive trees. What she would have exchanged to pluck a ripe fig and feel its juices running down her chin. Closing her eyes, Medusa thought only of the figs and the groves as a new pain roiled through her body. This must be death, she thought, as the sensation rippled through her, rushing toward the top of her head. Noises like whispered gossip or leaves rustling in the breeze hissed in her ears. Her eyes continued to sting with pain. *Death will come soon*, she told herself. The Goddess would have granted her a swift death, at least. Yet death did not come. Minutes later, an awareness began to return to her body. Still lying down, Medusa lifted her hand to her hair. Something sharp stabbed her fingers. She winced and pulled back her hand.

"I do not understand," she said. A trickle of blood had slithered from two tiny pinpricks on her fingertips. Hauling her body upward, she noted the weight upon her scalp. Once again, she lifted her hand and touched the tender part of her scalp once more, and once again, she recoiled as the pain struck her. Two sharp stings accompanied by four drops of blood. Her gut twisted, churning with an unknown dread. Twisting her neck, Medusa swiveled her eyes, first left and right, then finally upward. The sounds in the room dissolved into nothing but a sea of hissing.

"No, it cannot be. It cannot be."

EIGHT

MEDUSA HAD NO CHOICE BUT TO WALK UNDER COVER OF night, as there was no manner by which she could walk in the daylight. Even if she had kept to the shadows and walked only in the groves and forests, it would not be dark enough to conceal the curse that had befallen her. Errant rays of sunshine would surely break through and betray her, no matter how well she hid. Through brambles and thickets, she stumbled, praying that the moon would soon reach its newest face and be absent from the sky, for even in its muted pale glow, there was light enough to see the writhing mass atop her head: a crown of serpents fit only for the Queen of the Damned. They were bonded to her as a finger is to a hand or toe to its foot, and how many she had, she did not know, for she had not yet counted them. With every passing mile, she convinced herself that they would soon be gone. Once Athena had calmed down and seen sense, seen that Medusa was not to blame, the snakes would be gone.

The journey that had taken her four days with her father took three times that on her own. There was no one she could call upon to ask when she lost her way. No tavern she could crawl into to check whether the road she had taken would lead her to her parents' village. When voices rattled in the distance, she would scurry away, crawling beneath roots and between rocks to camouflage herself. She would clamp her hands around the snakes, pinning them to her head in a bid to stop their furious calls, while straining to hear the travelers' words, hoping to hear the utterance of some familiar village or temple. This was the way she picked her route, through the eaves-dropped gossip of merchants and traders.

It was on the waning of the moon that she sensed the eyes watching her. Six nights walking had seen her feet harden and blister, and while not a morsel of food or water had passed her lips, she felt no hunger. Just a burning desire to be home, in the comfort of her father's arms. That night was dry and still. Cicadas and field mice flitted about her ankles. The farmland she stalked held less coverage than she would have liked, with new wheat that was barely waist height. But the route was now familiar. Various craggy trees and a worn-down farmhouse sparked a memory of her trip with her father. She did not wish to lose the path and set herself back further by picking a more covered route, so she decided that if anyone was to appear, she would lie flat on the earth and wait for them to pass. She was just figuring out a place to rest before the sun rose when a single sound rang out in the night. Medusa stopped in her tracks, causing her snakes to fall silent in trepidation.

Yellow eyes glinted out into the dark, high among branches. Perfectly round pupils glimmered with a glittering gray. Despite knowing of its presence, Medusa had never seen the creature by the Goddess's side, yet there was no mistaking it. The Little Owl. Athena's owl.

With her chest pounding, Medusa's eyes locked on the creature, but it did not so much as blink.

"You know," Medusa called. "You know what he did to me. Why do you make me suffer like this?"

The owl offered no reply. It cocked its head to the side, then straightened it again. Medusa watched, her heart still trembling, as she waited for it to take flight. Even when she approached it and her snakes commenced their hissing, loud and violent, it remained motionless. A living sculpture on the branch.

"Please. Let me serve you faithfully, as I always have. Or let me pass on. Do I not at least deserve that after what I have suffered?" Time paused as she stood there, and although her eyes never left the little owl, her questions remained, unanswered. Slowly, the moon traced its path toward the horizon. Only when the sky began to lighten, and still no answer was forthcoming, did Medusa turn and continue her journey, knowing the yellow eyes would always be watching her.

After twelve days of hiding and twelve nights of walking, the boundaries of her family's farmland came into view. The owl had continued to drift in and out of view. Some nights, it would sweep past, casting its silhouette across the white of the moon. Other nights, she would only hear its hooting call off in the distance, reminding her of things she would never be allowed to forget. The Goddess had chosen her path for her. Now Medusa had no choice but to walk it.

When the farmhouse finally breached the horizon, the stars had already faded from the sky. Medusa's routine had been to find shelter as soon as the stars began to fade, but that morning, as the first rays of the sun struck the earth, Medusa knew she was too close to stop. The reward, she decided, outweighed the risk. The air was filled with familiar scents that grew stronger and more potent with each passing step. Meals cooked around a fire and the aroma of burning cypress consumed her. The feel of her father's hand—chalked and calloused from the ground—against her cheek; her sisters' heads against her chest as she slept. As she closed her eyes, all the memories seemed but a hairsbreadth away.

"The longest part is done," she said to the air, although as she heard the words in her ears, she knew them to be a lie.

Veiled from view by tall poplars and small almond trees, she felt her tiredness from the journey evaporate as, from her hiding place, she watched the family home.

A small figure skipped from the house. Laden with white sheets, she moved around the side of the building. Tears slipped down Medusa's cheeks as she held her breath. "Euryale," she whispered.

Her sister's hair had lightened in the years of their separation, her features grown sharper. It was an indulgence, Medusa knew, to come and see them like this. The kind thing would be for someone to weigh down her gown with rocks and stones and let Poseidon claim her for a second time. But what would her family learn of her then? That she had whored herself to a god and been unable to suffer the shame? She could not allow that ignominy to follow her sisters and parents throughout the rest of their days. What others thought of her, even Athena, mattered little to Medusa now, but she could not leave this world without her family knowing the truth.

"Nono?" A voice called from the house a moment before a woman appeared.

Medusa squinted in the morning light. Her mother? She had the same soft curves and gentle slope to the shoulders. Only her face, burdened with fewer lines, shined with youth. A shallow breath caught in Medusa as she realized her error. It was not Euryale who had emerged from the house, arms laden with sheets, but Stheno. Sadness and disbelief flowed through her. Had so many years passed? Her baby sister was now a young woman. Why did it come as such a surprise? After all, she herself had changed. A rasping laugh floated from her lips into the air. Oh, how she had changed now. Swallowing back the bitterness and treading lightly on the crisp leaves littering the earth beneath her feet, Medusa followed the line of the trees, making sure she remained concealed from her sisters.

With every sheet they hung on the line, Medusa felt the burning ache of separation growing sharper and sharper within her. Soon, the basket would be empty, and Stheno would go inside. The sun's heat would keep them inside in the cool shade, and she would be alone again. She should sleep, she reminded herself. Rest in order to face the task that awaited her. Yet she knew in her heart that she would not.

When her sisters finished their tasks and retreated to the house, Medusa kept vigil, unable even to close her eyes. Every sight, every scent—she wanted to remember them all, from the way the light reflected off the earth, to the feel of that same dusty earth between her fingertips.

As the morning heat gave way to the cooler afternoon, Medusa considered sinking down into the shade of the tree and getting some of the sleep she so desperately needed, when the cloth on the door billowed outward. There was no mistaking this figure.

"Father," she whispered.

Thales had aged. Possibly more than Stheno and Euryale combined. There was a heaviness to his shoulders that she had not known before or at least had not seen. Perhaps the blindness of her youth.

As her heart raced, the excited hiss of her serpents grew wild around her crown. She did not yet know what their speech meant, or if it meant anything at all. At first, each hiss had sounded the same to her—angry, vengeful, evil—and yet as the days had passed, she had come to hear the subtleties within them. The intonation. The rises and falls. She had yet to learn whether she had any control over them. Still, she tried.

"Quiet," she commanded. One or two dropped down, flat against her cheek. A sharp tooth struck against her skin. An accident? She could not tell, and for now she cared not. Silently, she watched as her father worked back and forth. All day, she remained there, transfixed, until the stars crowded the sky and the lamps glowed orange through the windows of the house. *It would be easy to spend the night hidden outside*, she thought. Then come back in the morning and watch them again. She could find shelter in one of the animal pens. It would not be hard. With a fierce inhale, she shook the thought away. How often had she spoken to the women about courage? Courage to speak out. Courage to seek help. If she could not take her own advice now, when she needed it the most, then she had never deserved her place in the temple the way she had believed. Bracing herself against what would come, Medusa took her scarf and wrapped it twice around her head, binding the snakes as close to her scalp as she could manage as they fought beneath her fingers. She would pay for it later, no doubt, but it mattered not. Not anymore. After this night, she had only one endless sleep planned.

With the snakes bound, as silent as the night, Medusa swept across the dry ground toward the house. With her hand trembling as she pushed aside the curtain covering the door, she called out.

"Father, Mother, I am home."

NINE

D O NOT OPEN IT ANY FURTHER," MEDUSA SAID AS A CHINK of light no thicker than her thumb escaped into the darkness.

"Who is there?" Her father's voice.

"It is I. It is Medusa."

"Medusa?" He moved again to open the door, but she clutched it with her fingers and held it firmly in place. "Do not open the door," she said. "And you must turn out the light."

"Medusa?"

"Please. Do as I ask. Turn out the light. Then I will come inside. Please."

A moment's hesitation hung in the air.

"I will see to it now," he said.

Thales's footsteps retreated, and the light of the lamp sputtered out. Adrenaline flooded her veins. The decision to come here had been selfish, she knew that, but there was no turning back. Forcing down her fears, Medusa pushed open the door.

"Child." Aretaphila's voice was weak and confused. "Is that really you?" her mother said and took a step toward her. Medusa shook her head.

"Please, stay where you are. You must stay where you are."

"But we can barely see you, child. I cannot see your face in the darkness."

Medusa nodded, even though through the blackness no one could see. Pain rose up between her ribs, a longing she had suppressed for so many years. Her need for her mother's embrace. She remained motionless as if cast in stone.

"Why do you come to us cloaked like this? Please, let me see you. It has been so many years. Let me lay eyes on my beautiful daughter. My beautiful, beautiful Medusa." Aretaphila's words became a sob as she moved for her child, but she found her path blocked by her husband's arm as he held her back.

"Medusa." Thales's voice trembled. "What is wrong? Why have you come back to us?"

In the quiet, she could hear the hiss of the snakes, incensed by their confinement. She wondered if her parents could hear it too. She had never been close enough to another person for the creatures to strike anyone, but she had no trust in them. They were not part of her, no matter how it might appear.

"I need to tell you." Medusa kept her tone as steady as she could. "I need to tell you both what happened. You must sit away from me. Then you may light a candle."

Thales moved deftly in the darkness, and soon, a faint glow began to brighten the room and illuminate the faces of her parents. Despite the desperate desire to look upon them properly, Medusa kept her gaze intently on the floor.

"That is enough," Medusa said as the room grew brighter.

In the dim light at the top of her field of vision, Medusa could make out her parents' hands. Thales gripped his wife's.

Thales gently guided Aretaphila toward the back of the room, although he himself made no move to follow.

"Father." Medusa spoke with longing. "Please."

Slowly, moment by moment, word by word, Medusa told them. She held nothing back, for she owed nothing to the Goddess. Nor to the other priestesses, none of whom had appeared to defend her honor in her hour of need. She told them about her encounter with Poseidon. Of the meetings before when he had come to her disguised. Of the night in the temple. Her eyes remained down as she spoke, recalling to them Athena's contempt as she had struck Medusa to the ground and left her bleeding upon the marble floor. By the end of the tale, her mother's weeping had grown so loud that she woke the girls sleeping beyond the curtain.

"Mama? Papa? Who is here?"

"Go back to sleep!" Thales spoke sharply to his daughters. "Your mother and I need you to sleep."

"I hear Medusa. Is that Medusa?"

"Your sister is with the Goddess," Aretaphila replied.

"But—"

"Sleep. Now!"

Her parents waited together in silence until no more whispers could be heard in the other room. Whether Stheno and Euryale were asleep, it was impossible to tell.

"My child." Tears choked the old man. "I have failed you. I placed you there to protect you."

"This is not on you, Father."

"It is all on me." He placed his head in his hands before extending his arms toward her. "Maybe this is a blessing. The strike she gave you, it cannot have wounded you so badly, for you found your way to us. You found your way back to us."

Medusa stayed silent.

"This is not on you, Father," she said again. "And this is not on me. This is on the gods."

Aretaphila shook her fist in the air. "They play at gods only when they wish to. Their spite, their vengeance, they are more grotesque than any mortal could ever be. I will go to the temple myself. I will demand an audience with that wretched goddess and call her out in front of the whole world."

"Then she would likely curse us both, Mother. And I will not give her that satisfaction. As Father has said, I am not dead. I found my way back to you. Maybe this will fade with time."

Thales rose from his seat.

"Whatever curse has been bestowed on you, we can weather this, my child. You can stay with us here. You will be safe here. The Goddess will not hurt you in our house."

"I fear you are wrong." Medusa knew she should leave then. She had said her part. They had listened. If she went now, they would remember only this. But the warmth of her father's words comforted her. Flooded her with hope. What if his words were true? If she could live out her days with her family at her side, should she not at least try?

She placed her hand on the scarf around her head, the coils twisting beneath her fingers.

"You should move away a little further," she said. "And try not to make a sound. I do not want to startle them."

Medusa knew her parents would be looking at each other,

wariness and confusion in their eyes. They must think she had gone mad, she realized, and she laughed sadly to herself. How much easier madness would have been. A mad daughter, kept in the house, let out only to collect eggs from the hens or to chase rats from the coop. Easier indeed.

The hissing increased as she worked on the base of her neck. She had penned them in well, and no doubt she would be repaid in malice.

Her eyes were closed as her skin endured the sting of their fangs through the silk.

"Before I show you this, please remember that I am still me."

The small candle seemed to burn brighter than ever. An overwhelming pounding had seized her body. The serpents grew more restless with every passing breath, and their nerves filtered down into her own, multiplying them further still. She wanted to wait, to wait until the pounding in her heart had subsided and the fear had lessened, but for that to happen even an eternity would not be long enough.

"It is me," she said, her head still bowed and her eyes fixed on the floor. "Remember that I am still your little girl."

With a sweep of her arm, she pulled the scarf away from her head.

"Gods above," Aretaphila cried as she collapsed into her husband's arms. "How can this be?" The rise in her voice shook the serpents, which hissed and spat, a writhing mass of scales and darting tongues.

TEN

MEDUSA REMAINED MOTIONLESS WITH HER HEAD BOWED, hands trembling as they clutched at the frayed tatters of her gown. Heavy tears dripped down to her feet as the serpents struggled in her mane, pulling at the skin.

"You see. This is the curse. This is what she did to me."

Aretaphila took a step backward, shaking her head. Fear was evident from her breathing.

"You must have provoked her. You must have misled the man. You must have—"

Medusa lurched forward. "No, Mother, no. I swear I did nothing. All happened as I told you." Her mother jolted in fear, freezing Medusa to the spot. "Please, I swear on your life. On Stheno's and Euryale's—"

"For the Goddess to curse you like this. It is not possible. Not unless—"

"Please…" Her voice was that of a child's begging for their parents' belief. "I did nothing. You must believe me."

"Hideou—"

"Aretaphila!" Thales's voice shook the air. His fists were clenched, the white bone of the knuckles glistening through papyrus skin. "Our child has come to us. She has trusted us."

"No, she is tricking us. Surely you see, no god would cast such retribution without reason."

The acerbity and recrimination in her mother's voice was sharper and more biting than the serpents could ever be. But Medusa did not blame her. When faced with a monster, who ever looked to see beyond the teeth and talons?

"You see," Medusa said as she clenched her eyes shut, the fear of seeing the disappointment in her parents' faces more than she could bear, "it is the worst of curses to have befallen. In all the history of the gods, have you seen anything like this?"

"Medusa…"

"Father, I am no longer a woman. I am a beast. A hideous monster."

Through her closed eyes, more tears escaped. She did not worry herself to brush them aside. Tears were of little concern to one whose eternity had been shattered. Words had finished. There was nothing more to say. In the forced silence, Medusa waited, although for what she did not know. Perhaps the prick of a pitchfork as her parents forced her out into the darkness. Perhaps, sharper still, a knife through the heart or across the throat. Her father had killed sheep and goats. He would know how to make it quick. As painless as possible, if they would grant her that small mercy. Her mother's whimpers filled the air. Was that to be the last sound she was to hear? What she wouldn't give for the sound of her mother's gentle song instead. Singing or laughter. She waited for the thunder, the screams, and the pain. Instead, what came was softness.

"You have been cursed," Thales said. "But it is not damnation."

He walked forward. He took the candle from the table and stepped toward his daughter. In the flickering of the light, her snakes stood erectly to hiss and bare their fangs. If Thales noticed their aggression, he did not show it. He moved beside his daughter and rested his palm to her cheek. The snakes moaned, low and groaning, whether of anger or pleasure, Medusa could not tell, for while they did not strike, they did not withdraw.

"You have been cursed," he said. "There is no denying that this curse is…terrible. You committed your life to the temple, and those whom you trusted deserted you when you needed them the most. But I will let you know this and hear this, for it is true. While you have been cursed by your goddess, I have been blessed, because you have been returned."

Medusa snorted. "I have returned to you like this, as a monster."

"When did a daughter of mine learn to judge people by the color of their hair?" Thales joked. "I thought I had raised you better than that." The laughter that he provided stopped almost before it had started, although a tiny glimmer of hope flickered in Medusa's heart. "Athena is wise, Medusa," Thales continued. "She will realize the error of her way. Believe me, my child. This will not be forever. When the time comes, she will return you as you were."

"But if you are wrong—"

"I am not."

"But if you are—"

"I tell you the truth, my love. I would bet my life on it. You served the Goddess with nothing but love. She will realize her mistake. She will rectify this."

Medusa's tears fell in heavy droplets, making dark circles in the earth, her shuddering breaths a constant rhythm masking the sound of her serpents.

"You are home, my daughter. You are home, and we will be with you." Cupping her chin with his hands, he lifted her head. Her eyes, glazed with tears, blinked until they cleared and met perfectly with her father's.

ELEVEN

THE SMILE ON HIS LIPS HARDENED AND FROZE THERE, SO
familiar and reassuring that Medusa had no choice but to
follow suit. Small but certain, her own mouth curved upward
in a reflection of her father's as she awaited further words of reassurance. One second passed and then another, yet none came.

At first full of optimism, Thales's eyes slowly lost their glimmer
of hope, while his hand, resting against Medusa's cheek, turned cold.
First his fingers, then down to his palm and wrist. Medusa did not
speak, for she could not fathom what she was seeing or feeling.

It was Aretaphila who broke the silence with her scream. "What
have you done? What have you done?" She moved toward her
husband, only to flinch back at the hiss of the serpents, her skin as
pale as melted wax.

"What have you done?" she said again.

Medusa stared, her eyes still locked on her father, her voice
stolen into a whisper.

"I do not... I did not... Father! Oh, Father!" She wrapped her
arms around him, only to find his body cold and hard. Stone.

"Father, no!"

The pain gave way to tears more acrid than any mortal could endure. They burned on her skin, blinding her again and again. "Father! Please!" She ran her hands across his body. His robe, his chest. Even down to his sandals. Stone, stone, and more stone. No fluttering of a heart or quivering of breath. There was no pulse, no life in his eyes.

"You have cursed us." Aretaphila stood with the candle in her hand. She held it outright, as a weapon. "You have cursed us all. You're a monster." The blood seemed to drain from Medusa's head and body. "You came here to our home and brought this upon us all. You are no daughter of mine. You are clearly a spawn of Ceto."

"Mother, please. It is me. It is Medusa."

"Monster!"

"No, please. I did not mean to do this. I did not know of this. I did not ask for this."

Earlier in the day, she would have thought it impossible that her heart could be any more broken. But this, her father's death at her own gaze, her mother's rejection, was more than any mortal should endure. A pain that shattered all the way through to her soul.

"You need to leave now."

"Mother, please…"

Without thinking, Medusa raised her head to Aretaphila. She wanted to speak. To plead. To cry. She needed the comfort of a mother's understanding. Surely, she understood. Medusa would not have wished this upon any person alive, let alone her beloved father, the single soul beneath the sun whom she loved even more than the Goddess herself. Anyone who knew her knew this.

"Please, Mother, you have to believe me…you have to…you… Mother… Mother?"

She realized her mistake this time, the instant it happened. Her eyes met her mother's. Even the dense well of tears could offer no protection. Before Medusa could scream, her mother, too, was turned to stone.

"No!" Medusa's knees slammed against the earth of the floor as she fell to the ground. "No, Mother! Mother!" Every cell in her body burned and screamed, the squeals of her serpents raw and rancid in the air around her. This was the end for her, for there was no more that she could endure.

A single sound cut through the night, causing the snakes to shrink back against her skull. It came again. The shrill, sharp hoot of a night owl.

A chill spread in ripples across Medusa's bare skin. Athena was here, Medusa realized. She had been here through it all. Watching. Listening. Medusa sucked down the tears that choked her breath. There was no fight she could win, not against the Goddess. Yet, what did she have left if not her will to fight? Prying herself away from her mother, she wiped the tears from her cheeks and lifted her chin to the sky.

"Is this what you wished for?" she called to the sky. "Is this how you punish me? These deaths are your doing, not mine." She waited for the reply. But none came. If this was how the Goddess wished to play, then so be it, Medusa thought. She was done with games. "These are the last lives you will take in my name," she whispered to the air.

Across the room, a knife glinted. Used for animals and meat, the heavy blade was sharp but aged, a red crust of dried blood soaked into the hilt. The curse would end now, Medusa said to herself. There would be no more death at her hand. The pounding of her blood provided a battle drum as she crossed the room and reached for it.

The serpents hissed, angry and loud, striking her wrist and fingers again and again as she took the object in her hands. They knew what she planned to do, but their instinct was to survive, not to succumb.

With both hands wrapped around the hilt, she lifted the blade upward. A final sacrifice to the Goddess, she thought to herself. One downward strike. A single plunge into her stomach. That was all it would take. Then the world would be free from her curse.

"Sister?" Medusa's mind switched instantly back to the room. The blade glimmered inches above her skin. Again, the voice came. "Sister, what has happened? Please tell us what has happened. Our parents, why do they not speak? Medusa, talk to us. We know it is you." The curtain wavered, fluttering from the pressure of the hand behind it.

"Stay there!" Medusa screamed. In her haste to turn, she dropped the blade to the ground. "Stay there!" she called again to her sisters. "You must not come out. Do not come out!"

Whimpers, so young and childish, floated through the curtain and pricked a heat behind Medusa's eyes. Unable to stop herself, she stepped closer, ignoring the fallen blade as she moved toward her siblings. Lungs trembling, she raised her hand and pressed her palm to the fabric.

"Please forgive me. I am sorry. I am so sorry," she whispered.

"Medusa?"

Through the fabric, another hand met hers. Warmth. Human warmth fanned out through the coarse fibers, burning up her arm and into her ribs.

"Euryale?"

Silence followed, as there was no need for an answer. "Father, Mother." Euryale spoke. "Are they there? What happened?"

Medusa's chest grew tight and she struggled to breathe. *What happened?* The question rattled around her head. What had happened? Nothing within her control. Nothing she could go back and change. Thousands of minuscule ripples had formed on the sea of her life and become a great wave that crashed onto her shore, decimating everything she knew and loved.

"I am sorry," she said. "I have been cursed, and that curse has killed them. I have killed them."

A stifled cry met her ears. Even the cicadas outside had diminished their chorus, plunging her deeper into the darkness. With a forced hardening of her heart, she pulled her hand away from Euryale's. To leave her sisters like this, orphaned and alone, would be monstrous. Still, she would rather that they remember her as the monster that killed their parents and deserted them than the sister who cursed them both too.

"I must go," she whispered.

"No!" The hand grabbed her wrist through the curtain, the strength and action catching Medusa by surprise. The serpents writhed up in response.

"I am sorry," Medusa said again, attempting to wrench her hand out from her sister's grasp. "I am sorry. I will send for our uncle. He will look after you." The heat of the night rose around her. With her sister's grip still firm, her own hands shook as she pried the slender fingers up from her wrist one by one. "I am sorry. I am sorry," she repeated as short, sharp fingers dug against her bones.

Stheno's weeping had grown more audible. Staggering breaths wheezed and hissed, scraping the air like fingernails on stone. Each sob was another dagger in Medusa's soul.

"Please. I must go. I must go. You are not safe here with me." Finally freeing herself from Euryale's grasp, Medusa looked again to the blade. Stretching down to the ground, she lifted it from the floor once more.

"Whatever happened, you are not to blame. I heard what you

told our mother and father," Euryale said clearly. "I heard every word. This is not on you. This is Athena's doing. She should have offered you sanctuary. Defended your honor. I pray that she be cursed for all eternity for what she has done to this family."

"No," Medusa said, dropping the knife, which stuck in the earth, and standing tall at her feet. "Please, Euryale—"

"She was meant to protect you. That was her job. That was why Father sent you there."

Her voice was full of malice now. The same burning anger that Medusa herself had felt. She understood it. But she could not allow it. Her mind whirred and reeled, the world spinning beneath her feet. Still, Euryale continued her raving. "You went to her for protection. You served at her temple and prayed at her altar, and now, she has stolen our whole family—"

"Please." Medusa was on her knees, eyes closed, grappling through the curtain to take hold of her sister. Fishing blindly around, she caught Euryale's ankles. "The Goddess will hear you. She will hear what you are saying."

"Good. I want her to. I want her to hear what she has done to us. She deserves to see the pain her selfishness has inflicted. What evil, unjustified—"

The scream that stopped Euryale's tirade was sharper than any Medusa had ever heard. It severed the night and sent the nesting birds flying and flapping into the sky.

"Stheno!" Medusa cried. Unable to think, Medusa pushed the curtain aside. Her baby sister lay writhing on the ground, clutching at her scalp as she wailed. A moment later and Euryale too was lying, screaming on the ground.

"No, please, no!" It was too late. The Goddess, as Medusa had learned, was always listening.

PART II

TWELVE

THE YEARS HAD PASSED SLOWLY. MORE SLOWLY PERHAPS FOR the burden of her company, now sisters in name only. Those first months had been the most treacherous. Fleeing the mainland, hidden under cloaks and shrouded by darkness, stealing what was needed, abandoning what wasn't. There had been death, both accidental and necessary. A captain, on that first day all those years ago, who refused them passage on his ship; Medusa had not considered any other options. She had simply lifted her gaze to the captain and informed an officer behind him that he was now the captain.

Later, on the same boat, an inebriated young man fancying the chance of a late-night encounter stumbled into the wrong cabin. Medusa had placed herself in the line of fate again. Better that the tally of lives lost to her rose than she risked what remained of her sisters' humanity. After all, nothing could burden her more than the death of her parents.

For the first months, boarding one ship and then another, Stheno remained swallowed mostly in silence. The only sound she offered was her soft weeping, which grew louder at night and diminished as the sun began its ascent. Her younger sister's body changed beyond the simple addition of snakes. Her spine began to curve, shoulder blades distending out at ungainly angles, causing pain when she moved and walked. Medusa stayed by her side every moment of the journey, offering words of scant comfort while Euryale continued to cast bitter tirades to the sky.

"She will pay. She will pay for this," she constantly muttered through the night, an acerbic lullaby for those she slept with. The same disfigurations afflicted Euryale as did Stheno; her spine curved as if an immense extra weight were pressing down on her back, although she showed no evidence of her pain. Not outwardly. It was one more thing to cast at the Goddess in anger. "She will pay for what she has done to us. I will see to it, one way or another. I will make her pay for everything she has done." One night, when Stheno was stricken with a fever, Euryale's wrath bubbled out into the storm.

"I will find a way. I will climb Olympus myself and bring a dagger to her throat. Do you hear that, Goddess? Do you hear that I am coming for you?"

"You should not anger her further," Medusa begged. Waves were smashing against the hull as the ship was battered from side to side. She held a soaked cloth to Stheno's skin in an attempt to abate the burning.

"Why? What more can she do to us?" Euryale lifted her head and hands to the sky. "Do you wish to kill us? Where are you now, oh mighty one? Finish what you have started, or I will cast on you a worse fate than your beloved titan, Prometheus."

"Stop your taunting, Euryale." The waves grew stronger, smashing harder and harder, and beads of water seeped through the planks, dripping onto the floor. "Stop it. They will hear you."

"I want them to hear me. I want them to see what their precious goddess has done."

"Stop it!" Medusa struck her sister with an open palm. The sting spread up through her arm. Euryale's mouth fell open, only to snap back together in a twisted sneer.

"Even now, you would side with her? Even after everything?"

"I am siding with you, Euryale. I am trying to protect you."

Euryale snorted in response, but her tirade, for the moment at least, had stopped. It would be better when they were away from people, Medusa told herself. It would be better when they no longer had to skulk in the shadows, listening to sounds of laughter and merriment up on the deck—something none of them would ever know. It would be better when they were away from the type of life they could never again be part of. And for a while, it was.

The captain of their last boat had refused to go farther than Cisthene and, instead, offered—for a price—the use of a small rowing boat. They launched at night, Medusa using a newfound strength to row them toward the setting sun. For three full nights and days, she rowed, never tiring, never growing weak, until, in the darkness, Medusa picked out the silhouette of an island, upon which she could see not a single light flickering.

"Here. We will make our home here," she said.

"There is nothing here," Euryale replied.

"No, this is plenty." Medusa plunged her feet into the water and began to drag the boat ashore, the hull scraping against the stones in the shallows. "There is shelter. There are some trees and, listen, is that the sound of goats?"

Even Stheno stopped her whimpering and tilted her head toward the island, catching the sound on the breeze.

"There are goats," she said, and for the first time, the tiniest glimmer of hope edged its way into her thoughts.

"Surely goats mean people?" Euryale's mind formed the same conclusion as Medusa, but she had already seen past it.

"No, I don't think so. I do not think there have been men here for a while."

Bending over, she picked up a handful of pebbles and shells from the shore. Like her sight and hearing, her sense of smell had grown more acute with each passing day. The scent on the shells was only of earth, of salt and seaweed, fish and fresh rainwater. And of something comforting. Safety from the world.

"I think we will be safe here," she said.

During the first month on the island, a rhythm formed. Euryale continued with her nightly tirade to the Goddess, while Stheno began to offer the odd word, sometimes in happiness, other times in grief. She would spend most of her time on one of the far outcrops, watching the goats, beckoning them over with her childlike noises. It was a caricature, this serpent-haired beast barely able to straighten her back anymore, huddled over like an old hag, calling to the goats with the words of a child. She whiled away hour after hour in that manner, although the serpents ensured she never got close enough to tame the animals. And Medusa, on that sparse rocky sanctuary, took up her mantle, the guiding ways of the priestesses still ingrained deep within her.

Under the moonlight, she would tell her sisters stories from the temple, of the people and the gods and the mischief they made. Her sisters listened, eyes wide, snakes silent. Only then, as the light of the fire danced in their eyes, was it possible to see them as a family of poor orphans like so many others. A family who relished each other's company and time. Stheno would lay her head down, often on Euryale's lap, but sometimes against Medusa's shoulders. These were the times when Medusa would feel a glimmer of hope. A flicker of what could be. The goats would grow used to them, she told herself, and maybe, when spring came, they would take a kid from its mother and raise it so that it knew the kindness of Stheno's hand. Then they would have milk and make cheese and spend their days as any other women might do on an island such as theirs.

Occasionally, during her tales, her sisters asked her questions about the time before the temple, when they were little. They asked Medusa what she remembered of them as newborns, as toddlers, favorite foods they ate, amusing anecdotes she could remember. These were the moments Medusa longed for the most, a chance to rebuild the connection that had been absent for so long.

"You must have tales that you can tell me too?" she would say after finishing a story about how Euryale had gorged herself on pomegranates until she was sick. "How about over harvest? Or at the feasts of the gods? Do you not have stories from then that you could tell me?" As always, she waited, heart in mouth, wishing for a glimpse into those years she had lost with her parents. But her sisters remained silent. The silence would swell and grow until the comfortable ease between them was lost. In the tension, the serpents would start to stir and twitch, lurching for one another. At these times, Medusa knew too well that no matter how many words Euryale spat at the sky, it was not Athena she blamed for their transformation. Medusa was the one who had sealed their fate.

Weeks and months turned into years, which passed with the same ebb and flow of the tide, the same wax and wane of the moon. New leaves sprouted green in the spring and fell crisp and brown to the earth when autumn encroached. They built fires, more from habit than need, as none of them felt as afflicted by the cold as they had once been.

The outcrop on which they had made their home offered enough greenery to stave off hunger, and enough caves and alcoves that some solitude from one another could be found. But at times, solitude from each other was not enough. What they longed for, what they all longed for, was solitude from the world. It was in the summer of their fifth year that Medusa learned just how much her sisters felt that need.

It had been a day to bask in the sun. One where the warmth that rose up from the ground was cooled and lessened by the breeze that swept in from the sea. She had been gathering roots and herbs with which to make a soup, grateful she had learned the difference between hemlock and cow parsley, given how close together the two grew on the island.

From her position on the ground, she saw the two figures approaching the top of the cliff. There was no denying the changes in her and her sisters, although rather than the physical maladies her sisters had gained, her transformation was more efficacious— another reason for Euryale's resentment of her. Medusa's sight had improved so much now that she could recognize a sea hawk from its tail feathers, a hundred feet from the shore. She could hear the rustle of its wings as they tucked inward, ready to dive, and the rush of air as it plummeted toward the water. Her senses had sharpened to the point that, even sitting deep within the network of caves, she could still hear the lapping of waves and the whistle of a breeze across the rocks.

The way the sun glinted, Medusa could have almost convinced herself—had it not been for the twisted spines and hunched shoulders—that it was any two women with brazen locks of hair, enjoying the heat and each other's company as they strolled slowly upward. Medusa watched as they continued their amble up to the rockier heights, gliding over surfaces where a mortal would have had to stop and go back, or else crawl on their hands and feet until they reached more even footing. For all their ungainliness, they too had a new strength that could easily have matched her own if ever tested. With their eyes on each other, they reached the highest point of the island and stopped about two feet from the edge of the cliff. Their manes billowed wildly, as though blown by the breeze and not the result of a cascade of serpents adhered to their scalps. Ignorant of Medusa's presence below, they exchanged a word before taking each other's hands. Medusa lifted her hand to them in a wave, but their eyes were not toward her. She thought perhaps she should call out and was about to do so when her sisters recommenced their stroll, this time at pace. Their snakes startled into the air as the two girls ran, hand in hand, toward the edge of the cliff, their fingers remaining intertwined even as the ground disappeared beneath their feet.

"No!" Medusa screamed, dropping the herbs she had foraged as she raced toward the beach. Bile caught in her throat.

"Stheno! Euryale!" Her feet caught on the rocks, causing her to trip and stumble. "Please. Please, no." She clambered up the rocks, her normal surefootedness failing her as her feet slipped on the greasy seaweed. Her knees sliced against the sharp clamshells.

"Sisters! Sisters!"

She heard the weeping, soft and muffled, long before she saw them. In her mind, she saw the injuries. Broken necks, perhaps. Shattered bones. *How can I help them here?* she asked herself. She could not. That was the truth of it. She could carry them back to the caves, maybe. But she had seen enough fallen bodies made worse by the clumsy hand of a helpful onlooker. They would die where they lay, limbs twisted at unnatural angles, caked with their blood. They would die, carrion for the birds that circled overhead. And she would have to look them in their eyes, fight back the tears, and hide the quiver in her voice as she told them that everything would be all right, even as the last glimmers of light faded from those eyes. That would be it. Her last sisterly action. To be by their sides and holding their hands when they died.

With a final heave, she pushed herself up to the last ledge. The air rushed from her lungs.

"How? It cannot be."

Huddled together near the base of the cliff, Stheno was wrapped in her sister's arms. Joints protruded at ugly angles, and sockets were dislocated and inflamed with purple welts. Despite this, their cries, she quickly realized, were not of pain.

"We will find a way," Euryale whispered, her hand caressing the snakes on her head and speaking as if a mother to her children. "We will find a way."

For Medusa, there were no words. She slipped down to a shelf below. Cradling her knees, she continued to listen to the muffled sobs and moans and vowed never to leave her sisters' sides again.

THIRTEEN

ESPITE THE PROMISE SHE MADE IN THOSE EARLY YEARS, IT proved almost impossible for Medusa to keep. While she never mentioned to her sisters what she had seen, Euryale, in particular, watched her with more narrowed eyes from that point on. The evenings spent together telling stories grew shorter. More cutting remarks interrupted her tales. Euryale's nighttime denunciations to the Goddess now spanned from sunset to sunrise and the hours between. She took to lying, sneaking off when Medusa's back was turned, often dragging Stheno with her. Stheno, who could barely stand now for the masses bulging from her back.

Once, they had tried to drown themselves; they walked out at low tide and waited to be swept away by the surge of the current. And swept away they had been. Submerged into the icy gray depths. Water had filled their lungs again and again. Spluttering and choking, their eyes burned from the salt as they coughed and cried and prayed for the end. But no respite ever came. All their struggles were to no avail. When morning arrived, their bodies, weak from the hours of floundering and sinking beneath the waves, were left basking on the shingled shoreline. Twice more, Medusa's stores of hemlock went missing. She didn't ask about it. She knew from the increased bitterness that emanated from Euryale during the days that followed that another plan had failed. The plans were all of Euryale's making, of that Medusa was certain.

"Why do you look at me like that?" Euryale asked after Medusa had once again found them washed up on the shore. Strands of seagrass clung to their scalps, tangling within the tangle of the snakes like a forest floor after a storm. "If you had any love left, you would have done this for us yourself. Slit our throats while we slept."

Medusa opened her mouth to reply, then closed it again. There was little she could say; it was the truth. But she would not be held responsible for any more deaths. Not in all eternity, no matter how much they begged her.

While Euryale grew more vocal in her bitterness and disdain, Stheno withdrew deeper into herself. She had lost her love of nature, of the birds and the insects that scuttled over the rocks. For hours, she would sit in the cave, scratching her nails against the stone walls, carving out divots in the rocks if not her own skin. Rather than letting the beetles and spiders crawl over her hands, she would squash them between her thumb and fingertips and smear what remained against the walls. Her body had grown worse with its ailments. Her joints were brittle and stiff, her knees weak and bowing.

"Talk to me," Medusa would beg, resting her hand on her knees and feeling the heat seep away from her skin.

"What is there to talk about?" Stheno replied.

"Anything. Please. Just tell me how you are feeling."

Her chin tilted, and her eyes moved toward Medusa. Where once they had glimmered with light and life, there were now nothing more than black vacuums.

"Can I still feel?" she asked.

The night the first heroes came, Stheno's pain was at its height. Her snakes stood on end, squealing out into the darkness, their cries echoing off the cliffs, filling the air with their agony. Euryale had disappeared outside, screaming at the winds as they blew in from the west. All day long, the wind had been howling fierce calls that whipped up the foam on the sea, although it had refused to break into a storm. Applying conjecture to her rudimentary knowledge, Medusa fashioned some primitive tonics and ointments that she forced down her sister's throat and applied to the sores on her back, which had now grown so large that they split the skin open. Slick with sweat, Stheno's forehead burned to the touch. Her words came out as choking coughs as her eyes rolled back and forth in their sockets. Medusa had seen a hundred fevers from her time as a priestess, fevers where the men's skin turned white and their eyes shined yellow, where foam frothed in the victims' mouths. Fevers where blisters broke out on their tongues and caused their bodies to convulse in pain. Fevers that she knew would break and find the patient well enough in a month or so, and fevers where she stayed by their side and prayed to the Goddess for a gentle passing. This was beyond even that. Water steamed on Stheno's pallid forehead. Her lips and cheeks drained white; her bloodshot eyes tinged with green.

"We just need to cool the fever," Medusa said to herself, for she doubted Stheno still had the ability to decipher words. "I'll take you to the water. The sea will help. Here, place your arms around me."

Kneeling to the ground, Medusa lifted her sister off the floor. With Stheno's body limp in her arms, Medusa picked her way down to the shoreline, placing her down in the shallows, where the waves lapped over her twisted body. The wind continued to battle as the first drops of rain began to fall.

"I... I..." A spluttering sound rose from Stheno's lips.

"Rest. Rest. Do not try to speak," Medusa urged. But the coughing continued until she finally choked out the words so desperate on her tongue.

"Kill me. Kill me," Stheno said.

The pain of a thousand daggers struck Medusa where her heart had once been.

"Shhh, shhh." Scooping water over the snakes, Medusa scoured the hill for signs of Euryale. The fact that she had chosen not to be with her sister at a time like this only served to show how far she had fallen. The last few days, she had grown even more distant. Like Stheno's, her afflictions had worsened, although she at least fought to hide it from Medusa.

The shallow wheezing of Stheno's breaths was barely audible above her groaning and the wind. Medusa leaned in to wipe some of the crusted foam from her skin when another scream shot up into the night. Medusa jolted, jerking her sister's head as the cry came again.

"Euryale?"

The screams grew in volume. At the same instant, Stheno's wails became a cacophony. From across the sea came the growling crashes of thunder. Rain pelted down, springing up from the pebble beach. Dizziness blurred Medusa's vision. The sand slipped beneath her knees while her own serpents rose up in protest against the sounds and rain that battered them.

"Stop! Stop!" Medusa cried to the air and to her sisters, neither of whom paid her any heed. Then she spoke to the sky. "Please, why? Why must you do this to them? Punish me. Punish me!"

Stheno continued to writhe in the sea. Medusa looked to the

cliff. There was no way she could get to Euryale. Her body, barely visible through the sheets of heavy mist that shrouded the island, was now on its knees.

"What do you want of me?" Medusa called to the Goddess. "What is it you want of me?" Yet again, she received no answer. "If you want their deaths, then just let them die. Please," she begged, her weeping muted by the discord around her. "Please end this." Her mind was still swimming with the sorrows of the years past when she felt a change in the wind. A chill prickled the hairs on the back of her neck.

"Stheno, be quiet." The urgency in her voice brought her own serpents to silence, although it did little to diminish either of her sisters' wails. "Please. I can hear something."

She swallowed. Her heart raced as she strained to make sense of the sounds that drifted beneath the cries from the other side of the island. Footsteps. That was what it sounded like. Footsteps on the sand. A dozen? Two dozen? Melodies of whispering tongues, the swish of armor, and a clang of metal. The sounds echoed off the cliff face.

Why would they come here? For the goats, perhaps? But then why the armor? And why come at night? No, there was only one reason men with swords would set foot on this island. To hunt a monster.

Steadying her breath, Medusa moved back from the breaking waves. If only Euryale and Stheno would calm, if only for a second, and allow her to hear more clearly. They would have to be on the east beach; it was the only place they could have dropped anchor without risking their vessels. It was a long trek over the mountainside to reach her and Stheno. But Euryale? Euryale would be right in their path. Trembling, Medusa shifted Stheno's still-burning body out of the sea and laid her under the cover of the cliff. The rain still struck and dripped down from the cliff face, and it was barely better than leaving her out in the open.

"I will come back. I will come back. Please, hold on a little longer." Medusa leaned down and kissed her sister. From the bare trees above, she snapped some branches and laid them across her sister's body in the hope of concealing it. If anyone were to find her in her current condition, they would have her head from her shoulders in a matter of seconds. Medusa needed to make sure they never got that far.

Fear and fury powered her up the rock face. A hundred yards from where she stood, Euryale was curled up in the same position as Stheno, clutching her body and writhing in pain. Medusa rushed to her side.

"Can you stand?" She hooked her arms under her sister's shoulders. "Please, Euryale. We must get you out of the open. They have seen you. They are coming for you."

It was true. From her new height, Euryale could hear the men coming, see the fingers pointing in their direction. Half a dozen were already on the sand. Another two dozen were battling the undercurrent as they waded through the swirling water of the shallows. One marched forward on the beach in front of the rest. He had a heavy shield in front of him, a sword in his hand, and armor over his chest that would have dragged any normal man to the ground. But he was not a normal man. He was a warrior. A hero. Even in the dark, his skin glistened, the salt from the ocean crystallizing into specks of light.

"Please, Euryale." Medusa felt the prickling dampness of her sister's skin beside her. Euryale did not move except to spasm in pain. Her serpents' tongues flicked out from beneath their fangs. "Please, we can hide. We can hide from them."

But even as she spoke, the words weakened in their conviction. The men had heard the screaming. They would not leave the island until they had scoured every last inch of it. There was only one way.

One way to ensure her sisters' safety. An image of her parents frozen in time formed in her mind. The captain on the ship. The amorous drunk. It was supposed to have ended, the death. Yet it was either these men or her family. The men had made their choice when they set foot on the island. Now it was time for Medusa to make hers.

"I will take him first," Medusa said to the wind. "Only the one at the front. If he falls, the others will surely retreat. There is no need to hurt more." She swallowed back the fear that had crept its way up her throat, and as silently as one of her serpents, she slid down to the east beach.

FOURTEEN

"WHY ARE YOU HERE?" MEDUSA STOOD IN THE SHADOW OF the rocks, her eyes and snakes covered by a heavy hood. "You are trespassing on my island. Leave now."

The screams of Stheno and Euryale continued to eddy in the storm around her. Lightning bolts flashed, illuminating the whole island. A few men flinched at the brightness, shuddering at the thunder that followed. Men or boys? The line was so close, and Medusa had never learned when the change occurred. She would think of them as men though. She could only think of them as men. The scent of weeks at sea was strong on their skin, and even from a distance, she could see the calloused hands of those burned by ropes and wood. She herself stood high on the rocks, her back to the moon, as she removed her hood. Her halo of serpents crowned her head as she called again.

"Why have you come here?"

In the moonlight, she saw his smile rise. He seemed younger than she. Euryale's age perhaps, but it was hard to tell his age and experience without looking directly into his eyes. Out in front of him, he swung his sword in a dramatic sweeping motion. It was all for show. There was nothing he could strike at that distance. Her vantage point offered her fair protection from the encroaching warriors.

"I have come for the head of Medusa, the Gorgon," he said.

"The Gorgon?" Medusa replied. That was what they were calling her. *Gorgos,* meaning "terrible." A knot of anger and grief twisted inside her. What a leap, from a respected priestess to a snake-haired monster. "I know not of whom you speak. I am a priestess. Alone here. Leave now. You will not find what you seek on this island."

As oily as one of her own snakes, the man's tongue flickered from his mouth and licked his lips.

"A priestess alone? Perhaps that is the very thing we have come here for." He turned back to his men, who jeered in support. "Perhaps our prize will be more than just the head of the Gorgon."

The air in Medusa's throat grew thin as memories of Poseidon's hands on her body seized her. The way he had forced himself into her, no man would ever do that again.

"Leave now," Medusa said, her voice a piercing hiss in the air.

"Why would I do that?" he snorted. The arrogance of youth.

"Because it is a better option than the fate that awaits you if you continue to advance."

The smile only broadened on his face. The jeering of his men rattled around her. "Where is your hospitality, priestess? My men and I are weary. Surely you can spare us a little of your time?" A shriek echoed in the sky, causing the man's grin to falter.

"There are creatures on this island," Medusa warned. "Leave now, and you and your men will go unharmed."

"My men can look after themselves," he said, approaching the shadows one sure step at a time. The drumming in Medusa's chest took on a new rhythm. Harder. Faster. Whatever the outcome, it would not be of her doing but by his own arrogance. As his footsteps moved ever closer to her shelter, she offered him one last chance.

"Turn back now," she said.

"Or what?"

This time, she was prepared. She stepped forward out of the shadow that had shrouded her. The moment she raised her eyes, she knew what would happen. The snakes coiled and hissed as she watched the arrogant sneer become sealed for eternity. The shock in his eyes registered a fraction later, just as the stone crept upward, his pupils turning gray, cast for all time in stone. Despite the storm, the sounds seemed to be sucked from the air; only the whirring of the men's brains remained as they attempted to make sense of what their eyes had seen.

"Back! Back!" someone called, stumbling toward the shoreline, only to trip and fall. "Back to the ship!" Yelling and shouting commenced as more and more men fought their way back to the vessel.

"Do not return here!"

Medusa sighed into the night, expelling the air in a gust. A pang of guilt struck her gut as her eyes fell on the figure in front of her. Another death. But only one. The rest of the men were fleeing, racing to their ships and away from her curse. Amid the chaos, a heartbeat of pure silence spanned the island. It lasted no longer than the blink of an eye, less even, and yet in that second, something had shifted. True silence. The screaming, she realized. It had stopped.

"Sisters!"

Twisting on the spot, Medusa clawed her nails into the rocks as she scrambled upward. Blankets of rain turned the rocks into a waterfall as she clung to them; the only thought in her mind was of reaching her sisters. Euryale first, it would have to be. But Stheno. Her darling Stheno. Halfway up the rock face, she heard a new sound that brought her scrambling to a halt.

The beating of wings was stronger than that of any eagle she had heard above the island. Hard and fast, they fanned the rain, pushing it to the earth in unending torrents. Their call was like none she had heard before, lower in pitch than a bird's but higher than a beast's. It had a nasality to it, as if the lungs of the creatures were filled with water. She cast her gaze upward.

"How?" The words left her lips before she could stop them. Even without the crowns of serpents, she would have recognized them. "Sisters?"

They were beautiful. Free. All the pain of the years forgotten as they glided through the sky, backlit by the lightning, blue-white against their wings. Dipping and diving, as elegant as swallows, they called out to each other. Relief at their freedom washed over Medusa, like water from a fountain. They were not birds; they were so much more. Lightning flashed then lingered, turning the whole night to day. Medusa gasped. The amber hues of their eyes had been replaced with swirls of green and red, their childish complexions now ravaged by pits and warts.

As she watched them, their aerial acrobatics slowed. Rather than diving and swooping, they took instead to circling. Heavy wingbeats echoed as they marked out a single path in the sky, around and around, eagles seeking out the weakest lamb to pluck from the flock before they all began to scatter. The priestess understood what was to happen the instant before it did.

"No!" Medusa leaped from her perch, down onto the sand, racing toward the boat. Even at her speed, she was no match for her sisters now. Each dive saw one, then another man cast into stone.

The sisters' laughter, grating and hoarse, crackled through the air. "They are leaving! They are leaving!" Medusa stormed into the waves that broke icy on her thighs. Around her was a forest of men, their eyes and mouths wide in fear. Her hands went to one and then to another. All stone. All frozen. "That is enough! That is enough! Let them go. You must let them go." She spun around, her eyes catching those of one sailor whose hands were grasping at the hull of the boat. In an instant, he was turned to stone too. "Please! That is enough!"

By the time her sisters had finished, there was not a single man left alive. Those who met their fate in the shallows had toppled and crashed down, fragments of their features now pebbles on the seafloor. Others had met their demise on the boat, their increased weight causing the bow to sink down. Another storm and the wreckage would be unsalvageable. Medusa sat on the shore until the sun splintered across the horizon.

When she returned to her cave, her sisters were curled up, their feathered wings swept around their bodies, blankets for their broken souls. The sadness in Medusa's own cemented as she noticed that, for the first time since they had been reunited, Stheno slept with a smile upon her face.

FIFTEEN

KING ACRISIUS OF ARGOS PACED THE THRONE ROOM. HIS hand trembled, and the air in his lungs stabbed sharply beneath his ribs. At his feet, the child giggled. He recoiled at the sound. His wife, Eurydice, in turn, recoiled only at him.

"What else can I do?" He spoke to his wife. "Death would be best. Now, while she is young. Our memories of her are precious and untainted. Surely it would be gracious to remember her in that manner?"

"Gracious? Is your mind addled?"

Eurydice rose from her seat, the anger glowing in her cheeks. She lifted the child from the ground and handed her to the nursemaid beside her.

"Take her to her room," she said. "Let no one enter but me. No one. The king included."

The nurse paled. Only a moment ago, her eyes had simmered with the same burning anger as Eurydice's, but that anger flashed to fear. To disobey the king's order would save no one. It would likely result in more deaths, particularly her own. Quivering and drained of color, she scurried from the room, child in arms.

"Acrisius." Eurydice's voice quivered. "Listen to me now. And listen carefully." Before the birth of her daughter, she had been fond of children, as was expected of a woman betrothed to a king. She cooed sufficiently and played chase with her friends' young offspring, generally enjoying the activities and their company, for a while at least. She could imagine herself having one of her own at some point too, but until that moment had arrived, she could never have anticipated just how much it would change her. But with Danaë's birth, a fire had awoken within her. From the first second that she held her daughter to her breast, smelling her sweet scent, her world had been transformed. All her thoughts were consumed with concern for the child, and her chest burned so fiercely that she laughed at her own audacity to have considered that she had some understanding of love before. This love, this bond, this fire that raged within her, refused to be extinguished, despite whatever prophecies were laid before them.

"You will not touch a hair on our child's head," she said.

Acrisius glowered down at his wife.

"Although she will murder me? You heard the Oracle's words. Danaë's son will bring about my death."

"She is but two years old. You expect her to bear a child now? Even if the Oracle's words are true—"

"The Oracle's words are true. She speaks only the truth. The child will be responsible for my death."

"Your kin will be responsible. Your *grandson* will be responsible. The Oracle spoke not of Danaë. How do you know there is not some bastard of yours running around in the cornfields now? Every king should have a dozen by now."

A ridge of fury stretched along Acrisius's forehead. "You know that I have never lain with another woman. That I never will. You are my love, Eurydice."

Softening, Eurydice lowered her gaze. A familiar throb returned to her chest. This was her weight to bear, not her daughter's. If only she could have provided Acrisius with an heir, with a son, he never would have found himself at the mercy of the Oracle's tongue. She stepped forward and clasped her hands around her husband's.

"I understand your fears, my king. I do. But she is a baby. She can no more bear a son than you and I lay a hen's egg."

"But she will."

"Then, at that age, we will speak of it again. But not until that age."

"Eurydice…"

"Not until that time, Acrisius. Not until that time."

That time came when she was fourteen years old.

Eurydice and Acrisius had grown apart, each unable to conceal their harbored thoughts about their daughter. Eurydice's thoughts were ones of fear and love; Acrisius's were of fear alone. Danaë had grown. Free-spirited, she would race along the shoreline with the local children, catching crabs on lines with fetid bait. While most young ladies of her age and upbringing kept their faces veiled in public or sheltered themselves indoors, learning the skills of weaving and flower arranging, she pilfered bread and fruit from the palace kitchen and handed them out among the beggars and the poor she saw on the streets. With her golden hair and azure eyes, she possessed a beauty that caused chills to crystallize down the length of Acrisius's spine. It was not a beauty that could be tamed, he realized. Not a beauty that would become muted or dulled over time. Therefore, it was, in his opinion, a beauty that had to be confined.

"You cannot place her in a dungeon!" Eurydice threw her hands into the air, spilling a platter of grapes and sour apples. Her temper tended to get the better of her more frequently as she had grown older, although she cared less and less. The fruit tumbled around her feet. "She is not some scourge. She is not some prisoner. You would compare my daughter to a child of Pasiphae? You think she is no better than the Minotaur? She is a child. She is my child."

"She is not a child any longer. She is a woman, and soon men will come calling. And when they do, the Oracle's prophecy will come true."

"It is a wonder the Oracle did not prophesy that you die at my hand, Acrisius, for soon I feel it is likely to happen."

Acrisius blew the air from his lungs as a small boy hopes to blow a ship from the shore. One by one, he picked up the bruising fruit from around his feet before he moved to Eurydice's side and took her hand.

"I know it is difficult to see. But it is for her own good." His voice was soft and melodious as he guided her over to the window's edge. "Look at this world we have made, you and I," he said. "Look at our kinship. Our people, are they not happy?"

"You know that they are. But if you cage their beloved princess in a dungeon beneath the ground, they shall not be. You must think carefully, Acrisius, or our people shall grow fearful like those on Crete. They shall whisper and gossip, and stories will stir of how we too conceal a beast within our depth. We too will require sacrifices to keep the beast satiated."

"But this is not true." Acrisius had paled, uncertainty shimmering in his eyes.

"Since when did truth play a part in gossip?" Eurydice replied.

Her words were met with silence, causing a private smile to flicker within her.

"It will not take long for the city to be rife with discontent. We all know of the unrest in Crete. Would you bring that to our shores?"

Acrisius pulled at the beard on his chin, a sure sign of his self-doubt. A slight breeze drifted in through the window, causing Eurydice's hair to whip her around the shoulders. Turning to correct it, she kept her smile concealed within. She had played a good hand but would not count her winnings until all the tiles had been played.

"Well, what would you suggest?" Acrisius bit. "You will not let me kill the girl?"

"Of course I will not let you kill her. She is our daughter. We will contain her in the tower." Eurydice pointed out the same window that Acrisius had led her to. "She can live in the tower, away from the gaze and persuasions of men."

"How is that different from the dungeon?"

"How?" Closing her eyes, Eurydice drew the cool air into her lungs and placed herself there, in her daughter's future. Raw and torrid wounds gaped in her heart as she considered everything her child would be missing. Was it better, she wondered, letting her live out her days imprisoned? Held captive by those who were supposed to protect her? But it would be a life, no matter how atrophied that existence. "She will be able to see the sky," she whispered, eyes still closed, the heat of the sun's rays on her cheeks. "She will be able to smell the salt of the sea and hear the cawing of the birds above her. She will hear the sounds of the city below her. Smell the meats in the market, the blossom on the trees." She pressed the words with all the feeling she could muster. "And in turn, the people will hear her. They will know that she is above them, watching them. A guardian, not a prisoner. They will understand your burden as a father to keep such a delicate creature safe from the rogues of the world. This is right, Acrisius. You understand that this is the right thing to do."

SIXTEEN

DAWN REMAINED DANAË'S PREFERRED TIME OF DAY.
There was something about that hour before the world began to stir beneath her that filled her with a sense of calm. Sometimes, the day's arrival was tranquil, a single birdsong followed by another, then another, until the air around her quivered with their music. At other times, the new day would roll in on a storm, thunderous and deep in its tremor, with dark clouds that masked the hour and rendered the songbirds mute. Sooner or later, though, no matter how bright or muted, the sun would always splinter into shards as it breached the horizon. And those first rays of light would reflect off the walls of her confines and remind her of her place in the world.

With dawn came hope. Hope that this was the day her father saw sanity, the day he trusted her at her word and allowed her to leave this prison in which he had cast her. Hope that this was the day they discovered a bastard child on whom the Oracle's prophecy could lie or, worst hope of all, that if her father's prophecy were to come true, this was the day when her suitor would come and take her to freedom.

Her tower offered no windows from which to glimpse the outside world. Only air and light from the open roof, allowing the gods alone to view her and cast the elements down on her as they saw fit. In the summer, the air became humid and sticky, so much so that her clothes would stick to her skin, and she would cast them off and lie naked in the sun. In the winter, her breath would fog and crystals would form on the walls of her tower. Yet, despite this, she was still a prisoner of relative comfort. Still a princess. Never wanting. Passing maids or childhood friends who had run with her on the seashores and dirtied their hands together with her in the palace orchards would be slipped into the bottom of the tower at her mother's request and whisper gossip of the world below through the locked door. Fate had sealed her into her chamber, but it was she who chose how she responded. Time would pass, whether she wept or sang. And so, Danaë chose temperance and hope. Laughter at the shapes of the clouds, joy in the songs that reached her ears. Her father may have planned to steal years of her life, but she could choose in what humor she accepted them.

The summer had been long, and day after day she watched as the sun made its arc over her room and peeled back toward a horizon she never saw. Often, during those long days, she would find herself thinking of the gods, for they were the only ones who could view her hidden away. A new kind of serenity came from twisting yarn between her fingers, rocking gently back and forth as she did so.

That day, she was at peace. Silver-tinted clouds had lessened Helios's blaze, keeping cool her brass-clad tower. When her fingers were tired from weaving for the day, she moved across the room, fetching a glass of water before lifting herself up onto her bed.

Heavy-headed crocuses decorated her tables at her mother's request, the petals of purple and white glistening and vibrant. As she lay on her back, she watched the silver tint of the clouds deepen, although rather than diminishing to gray as she had expected them to do, they graduated into the softest of golds. Shimmering above her, they grew in luminosity and luster, until they were brighter than Helios himself. Danaë shielded her eyes from the blaze. There was a god above her. She trembled at the realization. Maybe one who had heard tales of her fate and who could guide her. A patron within Olympus, perhaps. The heat from the light grew stifling. Sweat beaded on her pale skin, and her cheeks flushed redder and redder.

"Please…" Danaë called out, although whom she called to and what she hoped they would do remained a mystery even to her. Her heart trembled beneath her ribs, her breath shallow and lacking in air. And then, as the blaze seemed fit to burn her skin, the clouds burst, setting forth sheets of golden rain.

Through the opening above, the rain poured in great golden droplets, more lustrous and more alluring than all of her father's treasures combined. Danaë lay back on the bed, spreading her arms and legs wide on the sheets. Every place a raindrop fell felt as alive as if it had been kissed by Zeus himself. She opened her hands and mouth, tilting back her head as she allowed the rain to flood over her, soaking into the skin, and deeper still, until every muscle of her frame was tinged with its delicate light. Every cell in her body shook. Only when she was drenched in sweat, panting, did the shower lift. Still gasping, Danaë closed her eyes. When she awoke, her room was dry, the sky as cerulean as she had ever known.

It took two moons before Danaë realized the effects of the golden rain. Now, within her, she bore the consequence of that day. Fear and love wavered back and forth in her mind. If this child was born a boy, nothing other than his death would satiate her father's desires. And the child would be a boy. She knew enough about the gods to understand that.

So, she promised to love the baby in her womb, more than any woman had loved an unborn child in all of time. If these were the only moments they were to have together, she would treasure them, cling to every one. Every fluttering kick, every twist and turn. She would recall them all. Keep each one safe in her memory. Each day, she sang to him, hours at a time. She told him stories from her childhood and stories from her imagination, all in the hope that this would be enough for her voice to move on with him into the afterlife. And she named him. He would be the one to end her solitude and bring her back to the light. Perseus.

SEVENTEEN

IT HAPPENED JUST AS THE DAY BROKE. THE LAST THREE NIGHTS, IT had come in a similar fashion, rippling through her swollen belly, tensing and throbbing as pulsing surges brought tears to her eyes, but each time they had faded again by the time the sun rose. However, that night, there was no fading. By the time the dawn chorus had begun, Danaë's skin was slick with sweat, the ripples through her belly now great tides, waves, crashing down with all their force. She steadied herself against the wooden frame of her bed and bit down on the leather strap of the girdle with which she had secured her belly for so many months.

The child of a god. The child of Zeus himself, she knew, for no other could have come to her as he did. She would not scream. She could not. For weeks now, she had prayed her son would arrive in the night, when she could hold him and hide him. Delay his being seized and taken away a little longer. But the morning was the worst time of all. Soon, one of her maids would come with milk and honey and fruit for her breakfast. And only now had she learned of her naivety. The stench in the room, the blood that was dripping from her body. There would be no hiding this.

With her teeth clamped down on the strap, another surge swept down. She knew this was the time. This was when she would meet her child.

Breathless, she lay with him pressed against her. His skin was pink and smothered in the milky whiteness from his journey into the world. Her body throbbed, ached, and burned inside and out, yet, as he silently suckled from her breast, the pain melted into the periphery of her consciousness. All the times she had spoken to him while he was cocooned inside of her, all the words of love she had whispered unendingly in the silence of the night, it was only now she realized, just as her mother before her, they had meant nothing. Her life had meant nothing until now. This was love.

"Perseus," she whispered, over and over again. "My darling Perseus." Outside, the sound of footsteps at the base of the tower broke the false reality of calm. With a quickened pulse, she glanced around the room. Bloodstained sheets were draped across her bed. Cradling the baby in her arms, she lifted herself to her feet, only to drop back to her knees. The key sounded in the lock.

"You cannot come in!" Danaë's voice cracked. "You must fetch my mother. My mother. I need her."

Silence. Uncertainty as to which maid had been assigned to her that day.

"I am still a princess of the palace." Danaë held Perseus to her chest, praying her shouts did not cause him to cry. "I am ordering you to fetch the queen. If you do not, both she and the king will hear of this." The moment elongated, followed by the brief clinking of the key being removed.

"Certainly, my lady." The voice trembled back.

"My child!" Eurydice said, falling to the floor as she clasped her child and grandchild. "How?"

"A gift from the gods. From Zeus himself," Danaë repeated, knowing it to be true. "You will help me? You will help me bring him from here?"

Her mother paled.

"You should have told me before now." She rose from her daughter's side to pace the confines of the tower room. "I need time. There are people, but I need time." Her pacing quickened, her knuckles white as she clenched and unclenched her fists. "Your father rides out to hunt this afternoon. You must stay here until then, but we must have you gone before he returns this evening. I will go. I will find us a boat. I will—"

The door to the room swung open. A young maid, with a pail and mop in her hand, stood there. The fraction of time passed like an eon. The maid's casual submissiveness was followed by confusion as her eyes widened at the sight in front of her. Finally, the flush of fear. The queen leaped across the chamber to her.

"Go!" she shouted but an inch from the young girl's face. "Go now, and you will speak to no one about what you have seen here. You understand?" She gripped the girl's arm, causing the mop to slip from her grasp. "You will speak to no one, or it will be the end of you. Do you hear me?" The girl nodded mutely, tears building in her eyes as she reached back down for her mop.

"Yes, my queen. I understand."

"Leave us!"

Eurydice slammed the door before turning back to Danaë. Her hands trembled so much that they shook her gown.

"She will not stay silent."

"But—"

"She will not. You need to leave now. You need to come with me. I will fetch you a coat and gold. We will head to the harbor. Someone will take you."

"But, Mother…" Danaë clutched Perseus against her skin, praying for the sanctuary that came when he had been inside her. Eurydice was already back at the door.

"Open for no one. No one but me."

"What if Father comes?"

"You open for no one but me," she repeated, and then, after a moment's hesitation, she hurried back to her daughter and landed a kiss upon her grandson's pale hair before disappearing back into the palace.

They made it as far as the beach together. Eurydice had sent her most trusted friend to seek out a captain who would be willing to take a passenger on board with no questions asked. He would need to leave immediately and would be heavily compensated. Discretion was paramount. One was found quickly, and Danaë immediately prepared to set sail.

Wrapped in a cloak of wool, Danaë wore the clothes of a local as she edged down the steps of her tower and out across the court-yard toward the shore. The horizon was barely in view when she saw her father, Acrisius, waiting for her, an army of men at his side. Either the friend or the captain was less trustworthy than Eurydice had believed.

"You have lied to me." He spat the words at his wife.

"My love, you must understand—"

Acrisius stepped forward and struck his wife with the back of his hand. Eurydice and Danaë gasped in unison as the older woman was knocked sideways, blood spilling from her split lips onto the gray-gold pebbles of the beach.

"Mother!" Danaë screamed, but she could make no move for her. She had barely taken a step when she was seized from behind. She wrestled against the hold, fighting to keep the newborn Perseus in her arms.

"I wanted to save you. I wanted to save you from this, Danaë." Acrisius spoke with a tone of confusion as if he were the sole wronged being, while his bleeding wife and weeping daughter stood by. "If you could have just obeyed me. If you could have simply listened."

"Do not take him from me. He is the son of Zeus!" Tears streamed from her cheeks as Danaë clutched a wailing Perseus to her skin. "He is the son of Zeus. Please, do not take him from me."

"I should have spared you all the pain."

"Father, you will be punished for this. You will be punished for harming the son of Zeus!" The tears were salty on her lips as she spat out her words. "Do not take him from me. Please, the gods will punish you."

Waves crashed at the shoreline, boats pitching back and forth as white foam thrashed at the hulls. *He will get another man to do it,* Danaë thought as she was pushed to her knees, still clinging to her child. He would not perform the act himself. She considered later that, had Perseus been a normal, mortal baby without the blood of Zeus in his veins, he might well have died from the force of her embrace as she clutched him to her. Fervent, fearful, she would not and could not have let go. Holding Perseus to the end was all that mattered, making every second with him one of warmth, one of feeling his mother's heartbeat. Her father would not do this himself, she thought again as she looked at him. No matter what the Oracle had predicted. Killing his own grandchild was barbaric even beyond his level. Spears and knives glinted in the gray light of the approaching storm. Any of his footmen could be the one to cast the final blow.

Danaë was imagining their last moments when her eyes fell upon the chest lying in the sand behind her father and the armored men. The dull wood had not been sanded or polished like the hull of a ship, and its coarse, matte edges looked more suitable for a farmer's store or a place to hold clothes in the servants' quarters than to survive the elements out at sea. Beside it sat a pile of chains and heavy padlocks, strong enough to seal a vault. Dread prickled her skin.

"Father," she whispered.

"You may have your wish," Acrisius said with somber enunciation. "He will not be taken from you."

They took them out to sea, no doubt afraid that the fetid, bloated remains of Acrisius's handiwork could wash back up upon his own shores if not taken far enough away. She did not scream or bang on the sides to be let out. There was little point. She would not have the last hours of her son's life as ones in which he heard only screaming and anguish. Instead, she sang to him every song she could ever remember hearing as a child. Silent tears ran down her cheeks as she recalled verse after verse. Perhaps the rules were different for half-gods, she prayed. For he would get no proper burial this way. No obols to pay Charon for passage across the Acheron. There would be no crossing to Hades for either of them. The thought caught in her chest. *What kind of fate is that for a baby? He is the son of Zeus,* she thought as she attempted to comfort herself. Surely, he would be protected. That was what mattered the most. That Perseus was protected.

In her dark confines, Danaë had just grown used to the sway of the ship when she felt her motion change.

"Drink," she said, holding Perseus to her breast. "Drink and go to sleep, my love. It's time for us to go to sleep."

EIGHTEEN

PERSEUS MARCHED FROM ONE WALL TO ANOTHER. HIS BELLY was full of rage, rage that he directed at them all.

"You never thought that we had the right to know?" He spoke the words to Dictys. "Eighteen years, you called me a son. For eighteen years, I trusted you. And we hear this now, not from your lips but from his. Tell me then—if he had not shown his face at this house, would we ever have known you were a brother to the king of Seriphos? Brother to that vile tyrant, Polydectes?"

His words and rage were met by silence, which only served to infuriate him more. Over the years, Perseus had grown, and the house in which he had lived on the island of Seriphos had been spacious enough. Always, he had found room in this home to sing, to play, and to gut the fish that he caught with Dictys on the boat. This day, however, the walls had closed in, pushing him closer and closer to those from whom he wished to move farther away.

"Perseus, my boy, the king is not part of my world, and I am not part of his," Dictys said when he eventually spoke. "Yes, we are related by blood, but you and your mother are more family to me than he ever was or will be."

The answer did little to satisfy Perseus, so he turned to his mother. "Did you know, Mother? Were you party to this secret?"

"Not until I told Dictys that I had been sent word of the king's interest in me."

"Then why are you not mad? Why? This man whose roof you live under, he lied to you, and you do not feel anger at this?"

Danaë tilted her head and frowned. "You wish me to show anger? How?" she asked. "How can I show anger to Dictys, who plucked two half-drowned children, one but a few days old, from the shore and gave them a new life, or to Clymene, who raised my child as her own and was a mother to me when mine couldn't be?" Perseus pouted at her lack of allegiance, although Danaë was not yet finished. "You wish me to question those who never questioned me. Or you. Trust does not require answers, Perseus. Trust requires acceptance."

Perseus pursed his lips and glowered.

"Only now do we find out that Dictys is the brother of a king."

"And I am the daughter of one. And you are the grandson of one. Dictys has never lied to you. Never did he force me to disclose all the lurid tales of my past, and never once did I expect him to do the same. The life we have had is because of him, Perseus. I did not raise you to show such disrespect."

Perseus folded his arms across his chest.

"This cannot happen. You cannot marry Polydectes."

"Perseus, please, he merely wishes to meet with me."

"He will try to lay a claim on you. I know he will, Mother. I can feel it."

"Perseus, you cannot fret about a future that may never happen."

He felt as though he were talking to a simpleton. That his words would have been as much use spewed at the men who sat cross-legged by the ports, brains addled with wine, jabbering of the time they fought Ares in their youth. Enraged further by his mother's calm, Perseus turned his anger on Dictys.

"Tell me then, Father-who-has-never-lied. What kind of husband would the great King Polydectes make for my mother? A fair one? A just one? Would he be like you and never raise a fist? Tell me, Dictys. What will this marriage entail for my mother? What right does he have to come here and claim any woman he chooses?"

The old man's gaze wandered from Perseus to his mother and back. To Perseus, Dictys had been an oak of a man. Strength drawn from his roots, unseen and unshakable. Yet there, in the diminishing light of the day, his leaves had withered, and his branches curled inward, gnarled and weather-beaten.

"I tried my best for you and your mother, Perseus. It might not be a union that I would want for your mother, but I have no sway over Polydectes. To him, I am a simple, contemptible fisherman, no more than that despite our shared parentage. If anything, I fear if I try to exert any sway, it would simply make matters worse."

Perseus left, his wrath still bubbling. His mother to marry this king? He would not allow it. The rumors of Polydectes's temper were older than Perseus. An insipid man who made up for his frailty with wiles and bitterness. And to be lied to, for so many years, by Dictys and his wife, Clymene, who at times he shared more with than his own mother. They had betrayed them, no matter what his mother said.

His mind was a stinging web of hurt and anger as he made his way to the shore. One by one, he plucked gray stones and hurled them into the gray sky and toward the gray and crashing waves.

Surely, as the son of a god, he should be able to put a stop to this. He was the son of Zeus. Brother of Athena. Surely, he should decide whom or when his mother married? He grabbed another fistful of rocks, flinging them farther and farther out to sea. Whatever it took. Whatever it took, he would see his mother safe. Such a woman would never be married to a tyrant. Not as long as he was alive.

NINETEEN

THE UNEASE IN HIS HEART HAD FAILED TO LESSEN. TWO MOONS had passed since he had learned of Polydectes's desire to marry his mother, and three full days since he had fallen into the trap the king had set for him. Three days had passed since he had mistakenly forfeited his life and sent his mother into the hands and bed of a monster. Even he wasn't naive enough to believe there was hope. Not now. Not after this.

"Please, Perseus." Clymene took a seat at the end of his bed. "Tell me, what did the king say? What did he do?"

Still, Perseus could not find the words to admit his stupidity. He had returned home without his mother; enough evidence that Polydectes had thwarted him, yet so far, Perseus had met all his adoptive parents' questions with silence. Only after more wine than he had ever drunk in one sitting before did Perseus confess what he had promised to King Polydectes and his mother as a wedding present. First, his revelation was met with silence; then there followed an outburst worthy of the Olympians themselves.

"You are a fool, child. A foolish, foolish boy. Why make such a pledge? What in the world could have possessed you?" In the eighteen years of Perseus's life, he had not once heard Dictys's voice so full of fury as he spat the words into his face. "Whom did you hope to save by this endeavor?"

"You would simply let him take her?" The wine slurred Perseus's words. "Let him take my mother like she is nothing more than a bull, fit for sale to whoever can pay the highest price?"

"What difference will this make? He is a king, Perseus. My brother will have your mother either way. Now he has added your life into the bargain."

"Not necessarily. It is possible that I will not fail. I am a demigod." His defense was meek. The wine swilling around in his belly was the only source of his false confidence. "I am the son of Zeus."

"And with your father's arrogance. Please, Perseus." Dictys raised a hand and touched the boy's shoulder. He slumped in defeat and old age. "Will you not think of your mother?"

"What do you think I was doing? All I am thinking about is her. She is the reason for this. She is the one I was trying to protect."

In hindsight, he realized he had played straight into Polydectes's hands. The invitation to the feast had come a full moon before. Perseus had wanted to decline, but even he understood that the simple tactic of avoidance would not work forever. Polydectes had already met with Danaë on more than one occasion, and though she had always dressed her plainest and tried her hardest to rebut his advances, it had been to no avail.

"He will announce that you are to be married," Perseus said the night before they were set to travel. "He will announce it in public so you cannot deny it without making him look a fool."

"I do not doubt it." Danaë had been so matter-of-fact in her response.

"Then why are you going?"

"Good grace can carry you a long way, Perseus," his mother replied. "Even with such a man as Polydectes." Perseus doubted it was true, although he stayed silent, merely out of respect for his mother.

The day they left, the house was empty. Dictys had been out on his boat since dawn, although Perseus believed it to be more for avoidance's sake than a need for any more fish. Clymene had taken a poultice of herbs around to the neighbor whose skin had refused to heal after a scrape out at sea, and she too had been gone all day. The house, once spacious, had grown cavernous, for it felt as if none of the words he spoke managed to make their way to his mother's ears.

"I will go." He tried a different approach. "I will say you are ill with a fever. We can keep you hidden that way. Like that old woman whom Clymene visits, whose fever has lasted since the last feast of Ares."

"Perseus—"

"You cannot go to a banquet of his. You know he will do this. He will announce it, and you will be trapped. Bound to this tyrant king."

"Perseus, my love." Danaë's touch was as gentle as a petal on his skin. "You are a strong boy. A mindful man, but you know so little of the world. I spent my youth captive in a tower."

"I know this, Mother." The roll of his eyes caused the flicker of a smile on his mother's lips.

"Well, then you will know that for those years, I believed I was forsaken. That the gods had abandoned me. That I would never walk upon the ground or feel the breeze upon my cheek again. Then I had you. My beautiful boy, I feared so greatly, for both of us. There are so many ways my story could have ended. My father could have chosen a knife above the sea and chest. We could have died at the hands of Scylla or Laomedon. But there was no knife, and the waters were calmed by Poseidon. We arrived here, where the kindest man on all the island took us in without question. From all my fears have come nothing but joy. I have birthed and raised the most beautiful of all Zeus's sons." Her speech stopped as her gaze lingered on Perseus. "Perhaps the gods will be kind to me again. Or perhaps they believe my time of luxury has come to an end. Either way, it matters not. I must do this. I must go to him. And I would like you at my side as I do so."

And so, they had ridden the length of Seriphos to dine at the table of Polydectes.

The banquet was unlike any that Perseus had ever experienced. Gargantuan tables of deep mahogany stained with lacquer were adorned with a myriad of delicacies. So many meats, of birds and beasts and fishes, of sizes and colors that Perseus could only have imagined. Before this time, he had thought himself a worthy fisherman, looked upon kindly by Poseidon and the Nereids. Now he feared he was mistaken; fish of that size would have broken his nets. The earth had given a full harvest, and Polydectes had taken it all.

"You will sit with me." Polydectes clasped his wrinkled hand around Danaë's wrist. It was a gentle gesture in appearance, although Perseus saw how the skin beneath his fingertips whitened from the pressure and how his mother's lips paled as they turned upward in a smile.

"You honor us, Your Majesty," she had replied.

Perseus, by contrast, kept silent.

Polydectes chewed his food slowly, carefully grinding each mouthful to a pulp. Every inch of his face that could be seen beneath the tangle of coarse white hair was crinkled and creased, with skin so thin it looked like it could be blown away by a strong wind. Despite his age, he laughed a hearty, full-bellied laugh that exposed his yellowed teeth and produced sprays of fat and wine that spread into the air around him and stuck to the hair of his beard. Perseus had been placed at the same table, only two seats down from the aging king, bookended by two young women. One had skin like marble and hair flecked with gold, which shimmered as though granted the rights by Helios himself. The other one's skin was the color of a roasted chestnut, and she had a pinkness like raspberries to her lips. At any other time the two women would have proved the distraction that Polydectes desired, but for Perseus there was only one woman at the table, and his eyes refused to leave her.

For years he had heard Danaë's stories of Argos, of how she had dined at feasts and entertained the wealthy of the island, but never before had he seen that side to her. He'd only seen the side that gutted fish, scrubbed floors, and cleaned out clamshells after they had eaten the contents. Any hope he had had of Polydectes becoming disenchanted with his mother was a dream, he realized, as she smiled demurely and drew the gaze of all those around them. There would have to be another way.

When the meats were removed, cheese and figs and olives drizzled with honey were brought to replace them. Since they were so much sweeter than any that grew on the hillsides beside them, Perseus had to wonder how a king managed to procure such items, although procurement, he had come to realize, was Polydectes's specialty.

When fingers had been licked clean of the nectar, and fresh wine was brought to the table, Polydectes drew his eyes away from Danaë and laid them instead on her son.

"Perseus." His goblet had been overfilled, and wine sloshed onto the table. A servant hurriedly wiped it away. "I hear that you are a son of Zeus."

Excited tittering erupted from the girls at his side.

"That is what I have heard," he answered without a hint of the animosity he felt. "Although my father has paid me no favors."

Polydectes frowned. "No favors? You are dining at the table of a king. Surely, the gods must play a part in such a fortunate fate?"

The pressure in Perseus's mouth caused his muscles to flex and twitch.

"You are right," he said. "We have been fortunate. We were fortunate to be housed with such a man as Dictys."

Polydectes snorted.

"Luck in the home of a fisherman? I am sure the son of Zeus could not be content with such menial living."

"Menial living has given us no cause for complaint," Perseus commented. "By all accounts, we are probably happiest among the simple pleasures in life."

Polydectes's eyes narrowed, a thought churning visibly behind his pupils. A second later, he threw back his head in a laugh. "Maybe the herbs his hag wife has put in your tea have addled your brain." He slammed his goblet down on the table, and more wine slopped onto his tunic. Guests laughed in raucous agreement—or, at least, the appearance thereof. In an instant, a man was at the king's side, refilling the glass and mopping the table. "Well, you are to be blessed soon, young Perseus. Stepson to the king of Seriphos. A great honor to be cast upon a forgotten bastard, is it not?"

In an instant, a hush descended on the room. Eyes that only a moment ago had been scrunched in laughter now flitted nervously, the flames of the oil lamps flickering in the stillness. A bastard son he may be, but he was still the bastard son of Zeus. If Polydectes saw the fury and fear flash around Perseus's face, he did not show it. This was the king in public, Perseus considered, biting his tongue so hard he could taste the spill of blood. This was the best face Polydectes could put forward for his new bride. The gods alone could only imagine how much more hideous he could be in the privacy of his own chambers.

"You approve, I assume," Polydectes continued. "This marriage for your mother—at her age—is a great blessing. An honor. She has found herself quite a remarkable suitor, do you not agree?"

Whether Polydectes's men were admirers of their king made little difference to the fact that they were his men. Guards with their hammered spears and kinsmen with concealed knives surrounded him, faces plastered in false smiles. There was only one answer Perseus could give.

"Naturally, what son could wish for more?" The reply was met by an unmistakable sneer from Polydectes.

"I have already been gifted two dozen horses as wedding presents. Have you heard of such a thing?" He pointed his question briefly at Danaë before returning his attention to Perseus. "To be gifted such things before a date for the union is even set."

"I only wish I could offer you a gift worthy of such a union," Perseus replied. "Yet, I wonder what gift that could be."

It was such a slight remark said with such ease and composure that, for a second, Perseus did not see the snare waiting. The wine-induced glaze vanished from Polydectes's eyes in an instant, his yellowing teeth fully visible in his sneer.

"There is one gift you can bring me," he said.

———

Words had been exchanged. Toasts were raised, and the curtain of impending doom had fallen on Perseus, as tangible and weighted as the cloak on his back. The head of the Gorgon Medusa was to be Perseus's wedding gift. The head of a creature millennia old who had murdered thousands of innocent men. His heart drummed at the trap he had walked himself into. He was to leave as soon as he had readied a ship. And on the day of his return, his mother was to marry Polydectes. That was what Polydectes had promised. Only, no one ever returned from Medusa, and the tyrant king knew this all too well. A simple plan to rid himself of an unwanted stepson. However, Perseus, perhaps naively, had hatched a plan of his own. He would retrieve the Gorgon's head as requested and then turn the wedding present against the king, freeing Seriphos—and his mother—from Polydectes's malevolent reign.

TWENTY

I N THE DAYS PREPARING TO SET SAIL, PERSEUS'S HEART GREW HEAVY
with his impending fate. In contrast, his head grew numb from
the wine he used to avoid thinking about it.

"You will take my boat," Dictys said. "It is small but sturdy.
And it's the best you'll find this end of the island. You will need to
find yourself a crew though. Six men should be enough. And choose
wisely. A man's temperament on dry land is rarely the same as one
who must endure storm after storm."

His stepfather had spoken with resolution and authority, as
opposed to the bitterness he had every right to. That alone was enough
to churn up even more guilt from the unending supply Perseus had
found himself possessing. No word had come from his mother, and
each passing hour without news only caused the guilt and fear to
multiply. Perseus nodded mutely to Dictys's instructions, the effects
of the previous night's wine slowing his rate of comprehension.

"I cannot take your boat." He realized he had not offered an
answer. "It is your livelihood. You need it. You will not be able to
fish without."

"Really? I had not considered that fact." Dictys smiled with a good-naturedness that Perseus was unable to reciprocate. "It is fine. We have enough for now. And with two fewer mouths to feed, what we have will stretch twice as far. Probably four times given the amount you consume."

His grin continued, and this time Perseus allowed himself the briefest smile, if only for his stepfather's sake. "It is kind of you to offer, but I cannot," he said, the smile already gone. "You need it. This journey is long. And if I don't… If I am not…" Perseus swallowed the lump that had lodged itself in his throat. "It is possible that I… you know." *Some hero*, he sneered to himself. Such a hero that the mere thought of dying was enough to slicken his skin with sweat. He forced his shoulders back and straightened his spine. "This journey may take many years," he said. "I could not allow you to go that long without being able to provide for yourself."

"Well, then perhaps I will take to shipbuilding," Dictys replied. "These arms have still got plenty of strength in them yet. I am not the withered man my brother has become." He placed a hand on Perseus's shoulder, his flippant manner gone. "Do not worry about me, Perseus. Clymene and I have weathered plenty of storms in our time."

Knowing he had no other choice, Perseus agreed to the offer.

His family's generosity did not stop there. Clymene insisted on plying Perseus and his men with all the dried fish, fruit, and grain they could manage, rousing the village into action to see that the stores on the small boat were full.

"It will be hungry work out on the sea," she said, looking at him with the same motherly tenderness she always bestowed. "And I know it is not a lot, but we have some pieces—some gold and silver—that you can trade if you need to."

Perseus shook his head. "I cannot take any more from you," he said, pushing the items back into Clymene's hands. Her eyes shined softly in the light.

"Perseus, we could give you every item in our possession, and it would still not be enough to repay you for the years you have allowed me the gift of having you as a child. That is the same for your father too. You know that."

The lump that had become a consistent feature in his throat over the past few days began to swell further, blocking the air to his lungs and causing his eyes to sting with tears. Still, he refused the gifts.

It had taken only a couple of days for Perseus to find himself a crew, and although eager, they were younger than he would have hoped for.

"It is no surprise," he said to Dictys as they walked together to the port on the arranged morning of his departure. "Anyone older is either with children and wives they do not wish to see widowed or merely sensible enough to know that nothing good will come from this."

"Do not lose faith," Clymene said, looping her arm through his as they walked. "Remember, whether we think of you as our own or not, you are the son of Zeus. You have the gods on your side."

"It would be nice to see evidence of such a fact," he said grudgingly.

By now, the news of Perseus's quest had spread across Seriphos, and as such, he was unsurprised to hear of a crowd gathering at the port. It would be a bittersweet farewell, he considered. The one brief moment before the event when he could bask in the glory that a real hero felt. He should enjoy it, he thought. Or at least pretend to.

Despite having heard the rumors of a send-off, Perseus was not prepared for the sight that befell him when he turned the corner onto the harbor.

"This cannot all be for me, surely?" The nerves and butterflies that had beleaguered his body since morning gave way to confusion. The crowd he saw was as big as any that would gather at a feast of the gods, with what appeared to be the entire island crowding around the water. At the back, many were craning their necks, standing on tiptoes, or hoisting their children onto their shoulders to get a better view, and from the hills, more still were rushing down to join them.

"I must get through." Perseus used his hand to push aside a man at the edge of the group. "I need to get to my boat." The man turned his head quickly, only to twist it back around and fish about for a better view of the sea and the boat. A clicking sound traveled through his skull as Perseus rolled his lower jaw from one side to another. "Did you hear me? I need to get through. My boat. My crew. I must make haste." Whatever the excitement was, it took Perseus only a minute to now realize that he was not the cause of it. "I am done asking," he said and began to elbow his way into the mass. Only when he had pushed himself into the middle of the crowd and found that the front half of the congregation had fallen to their knees did he realize the source of the furor.

"Brother, you have arrived."

The cerulean sky was dull in comparison to the way she shined. Clad in gray yet brighter than Helios, she approached him across the shore, her feet leaving no mark in the sand. "Make room. Make room for my brother," she spoke again, and Perseus felt the weight on his shoulders diminish and double at the same instant.

"Pallas Athena?" The name came out as a question, for he wondered how it could be possible that the Goddess of Wisdom, fiercest of warriors and patron of the greatest heroes, could be standing on the shores of Seriphos addressing him as her kin. Her eyes glinted. A moment later, he fell to his knees.

"Perseus." She reached a hand down and pulled him back up to standing. Her touch was as light as air, yet behind it all was the strength of an Olympian. "We should get going. Your crew is awaiting you." Then with a wry smile, she tilted her chin toward the ocean behind her.

Perseus had seen great ships before. Less than a week ago, he had been standing at the harbor of Polydectes's palace, and white clouds had rolled above him as he gazed half-admiring and half-belligerent at the king's fleet. He had thought about Dictys at the time. How tiny and puny his own vessel would look in comparison. But the ship before him now was something truly magnificent to behold.

If he ever did return from the voyage, this would be his gift to Dictys for his years of adoption. This ship. And with his hero's bounty, a crew who would forever be at the helm for his beloved stepfather. Beneath its towering masts, men clad in armor grasped at oars or else strode from one side of the ship to the other, barrels and ropes slung effortlessly over their shoulders. These were not the half dozen men of his selection, but two dozen warriors. Beasts of men. Perseus paled. As the son of Zeus, he had had no trouble taking strength for granted on such an island as Seriphos. Since the age of eight, he had been as strong as any man he encountered. This would be the first time he would have his lineage tested.

"We should board." Athena's words broke him from his thoughts. "Time is of the essence, I assume?"

He nodded, his eyes still transfixed on the ship for a moment longer. The wind picked up a little, causing the sails to billow and bulge. Perseus turned his head toward the gathering on the shore, scanning through the disbelieving eyes, all still gazing in awe at

Athena. His sister. Between the figures, he picked out the raised hand of Dictys. His heart tumbled over in his chest. If there was one image he would take with him to draw strength from, one image of the life he wished to return to, it would be this. With a knowing smile, his eyes met his stepfather's, and he offered him a single nod. "For your mother," Dictys mouthed.

"For my mother," Perseus said.

TWENTY-ONE

PERSEUS TOOK THE OARS AND ROWED FROM THE SHORE TO THE waiting vessel. His sister—she allowed the word to turn over in his head—stood at the helm, bare arms golden, gray chiton motionless in the breeze. No further words were exchanged as they boarded the great ship and took to the open water. Perseus watched the men, sweat glistening on their arms. He did not know from which island the men came—if they were islanders at all. It was possible they came from all regions of Hellas. No doubt a selection of the Goddess's own choosing. Perhaps there were heroes among them. Worthier ones than him, who would risk the gaze of the Gorgon. After all, Polydectes's only requirement was that Perseus bring him the head of Medusa. He did not specify that he must be the one to sever it.

"The crew is yours," Athena said as if reading his mind. "When I leave, they will follow your command. They know the route to the Gorgon's island."

"Then perhaps one of them should be in charge." Perseus spoke only half in jest. Athena noticed and smiled.

"And you would have them take the head of Medusa themselves too, I assume?"

The color of his cheeks betrayed his earlier thought.

"The Gorgon is old and wily; no mortal can stand against her," she said, saving Perseus the shame of answering her previous question. "Many have tried. None have succeeded. But only mortals; no sons of Zeus have attempted such an act."

Perseus cast his gaze out onto the ocean. On the horizon, a small smudge of land marked his final vision of Seriphos. He would return only if he succeeded. There would be no other home for him now.

The humidity of the air was broken by the wind that filled their sails. For now, the men's oars were superfluous, and they busied themselves about the deck. How long they would be blessed with good winds, Perseus dared not ask. Better accept the gifts of the gods and stay silent than risk their wrath by seeking more.

"The Gorgons," he said instead. "How did they become this way? Was it a punishment from the gods?"

"A punishment?" The most diminutive of quivers disturbed the Goddess's tone. "Why would you say that? What have you heard of their creation?"

"I only heard that they were born that way. That the three creatures are nearly as old as the gods themselves."

"Then why would you question it?" It was no longer a slight quiver in her voice. Her inflection was more of a blunt edge. A solid strike. The winds picked up. Men hurried to the forestays and fastened the sheets.

"On my island there is debate as to their lineage. Whether or not Typhoeus and Echidna or Phorcys and Ceto spawned the beasts."

"Does it matter? Your task, as I understand it, is to remove her head. That is all."

"Goddess, I did not mean to cause offense. I know that the gods are fair and just in their actions. I only wished to learn as much about my foe as I am able. That is what a good hero does, is it not? Learns their opponents' weaknesses."

Athena's face softened into a smile, although her gaze still held fast to the glint of distrust. Her lips pressed together in a line before she turned her head to the same smudge of land—now little more than a speck—on which his eyes had been focused only minutes beforehand.

"I can tell you what I know of the Gorgon Medusa." Her eyes remained on the ocean as she spoke. "I can tell you that millennia in isolation creates beasts for whom rational thought will no longer prevail. She may speak in the same tongue as a human, but there is no more humanity running through her veins than there is sustenance in the venom of the vipers that coil around her scalp. I can tell you that she takes pleasure in each death, toying with her victims as a cat does with a mouse. Of course, a mouse with a wounded leg may escape the cat to go and die in some hidden corner of a field on their own terms. There is no such blessing for Medusa's victims. No such moment of solitude." She turned her eyes back to Perseus. The gray glint was now gone, replaced by something darker still. "She is not human. She has never been human. Do not fool yourself into thinking otherwise. She will not fall for human trickery. She has seen it all and defeated it all."

Goose bumps had spread the length and breadth of Perseus's skin. "Then, if that is the case, how will I defeat her?"

"With this." Athena smiled.

TWENTY-TWO

Yet another hero soiling his tunic before he has even lifted his sword." Euryale laughed, kicking at the statue as she caressed one of the serpents that coiled downward toward her throat. Arching her back, she clicked and creaked her wings, then folded them down again.

Outside came the shrill squawks of the seabirds. The streaming patter of rain was unremitting on the island. Normally, rain stemmed the flow of heroes, but these boats must have already sailed too far to contemplate turning back.

"They grow weaker and weaker." Stheno prodded where the man's legs would have been, now hidden in a skirt of stone. "Pathetic excuses for men."

"This one made it through the garden at least." Euryale cupped her hand around his cheek, tilting her head as she surveyed it.

"Only because we allowed it." Stretching out her finger, Stheno carved a line in the stone with her nail where his heart used to be. The sound resonated off the walls around them. "When will they ever send us an actual hero? One that challenges us. Perhaps even manages to slit your throat."

"Mine? I think you would find that it would be yours they would go for first. Even a bad predator can spot the weakling in the pack."

"Oh, how you wish, sister."

Shrieks and wails erupted as the two Gorgon sisters grappled one another. Claws and fangs and scales flashed in the dim light of the cave. Each strike clattered louder and louder, shaking the small stones and gravel on the ground. The man was forgotten. In the struggle, his figure was struck on the torso with the flap of a wing. It wobbled, tipped, then fell and shattered around them.

"Enough!"

The sisters shrank back into the shadows, forked tongues probing the air toward Medusa. Over the years, she had grown impervious to their hate. It was deserved. Had she fled the house like she knew she should have after her parents' death, they would simply have been orphans. A hard life, yes, but a life. With a mortal span. A mortal end. Millennia had passed, yet the scars of her actions had still not faded.

"Outside with you! I need peace." In this cave, if nowhere else, she had her dominion. Even so, her words were met by a chorus of hissing. "Did you not hear me? I said outside."

She bared her own fangs, locking her gaze on Euryale's red eyes. In the silence, eddies of dust swirled around her. Outside, the drumming of the rain intensified. Medusa willed her snakes to stay silent, for to hiss and attack would only rile her sister more.

When Euryale finally spoke to Stheno, it was as if Medusa were not even present. "Come, let us see what the day has brought," she said. "Perhaps Father has sent us a lost ship." Her eyes glinted. Medusa forced down the caustic sting of bile as it bit in her throat.

"Perhaps he has sent us many," Stheno replied.

Father. They had taken to using the term for the God of the

Sea as a source of mockery—Poseidon's rape of Medusa somehow a source of comfort to them, maybe that she had at least suffered one indignity they had not. Over the years, their mockery, like their compassion, had faded, and now, when they spoke this name, it was in earnest. They praised him for what he brought them. For the heroes he guided to their shores for their entertainment. Try as she might, Medusa had no choice but to despise them for it.

With bitching words, the sisters fled outside, scraping their talons on the walls of the cave as they went. The sound of beating wings came as both a blessing and a curse. Often, they would disappear for days on end, sometimes weeks, months. One time, they were gone almost a full year, and when they returned, they spoke as if they had not even noticed her absence among them. After all, what is a year for those who have lived for millennia? Summers, winters, seasons are like the passing of a day.

She could have wished them away for eternity had it not been for the consequences that befell her in their absence.

Medusa did not mind being ostracized the way she once had. The company of her serpents, though wordless and writhing, was a greater comfort than her sisters could ever be now. But she missed them when they were gone. For without the two-winged Gorgons, it fell to Medusa to deal with the heroes.

For years, she tried to reason with them. To plead with the men who came armed with swords and daggers to end her life.

"Please, go back. Go back now." She would hide in the shadows and call from a distance. "You can save yourself. Please go back."

Often, they laughed. The arrogance of men did not allow them to take orders from a woman. Even one who was two thousand years old and capable of ending their lives. And end their lives she did, every time. She tried not to. For years she stood with her eyes closed, hoping that one would be swift enough to beat the jaws of her serpents before they sprang from their coils and pierced their fangs into her skin. Sometimes they struck the men too, but normally their fangs were aimed solely at their mistress. Neck, shoulders, the small patch of soft flesh that still remained behind her ears—they knew the exact position that would force her eyes to spring open on reflex. Every time, their ploy had worked, and every time, whoever her gaze landed upon was condemned to an eternity of stone. She tried with blindfolds, fashioned from the scraps of material that had snared on rocks as men retreated, but again, the serpents refused to allow it, tearing the cloth with their teeth until only fibers remained.

She would have tried death from the sea, like her sisters, but she knew that Poseidon would never grant her such a luxury. A fall from the cliffs, she suspected, would be saved by some miracle of the gods. She was, as she had always been, at their mercy.

So now, when her sisters left, she waited for the heroes to come by, holding a vigil out in front of the cave, on the small patch of greenery her sisters referred to as the garden. A swift death, as little fear as possible—that was all she could offer them now.

TWENTY-THREE

THE DAYS AT SEA HAD TRANSFORMED HIM INTO A DEMIGOD deserving of the name, although it had not come without hard work and sweat. Athena had placed among his crew two warriors from Sparta, one slight man, whose feet moved more nimbly than those of a cat, the other almost double the size and able to throw a man like Perseus with one hand. For hours each morning, while his crew tended to the ship, Perseus would spar with them. Day after day, through storms and blistering sun, he endured blow after blow as he sought the skills that had taken them years to possess. Each morning, they would be up before Perseus had risen, ready to administer their lessons. His skin would split again and again. His legs, his shoulders, no part of his body was immune to their weapons. His knuckles grew hard and strong, and his palms calloused and scarred as, time and again, he was disarmed and forced to battle with his hands alone. His nose, he feared, would never know its birth-given shape again. He went to bed with limbs aching, purpled with bruises and brown with dried blood, and he woke each morning ready to train harder still.

It did not take long before he decided on the xiphos as his weapon of choice. The sound of the double-edged sword slicing through the air became to him as rhythmic as the oars against the sea. The dull thud as it struck his opponent's armor—more and more frequent with every day that passed—as melodic as the mistle thrush. He grew faster, stronger, more agile. He learned to read his two opponents' moves, a twitch of the thigh, a flick of the finger. Soon, he was asking other members of the crew to join them. To even the field. Three, four, five on one. Soon, Perseus could take all of them on.

Time spent away from training he spent learning.

"Which island is that?" he would ask the men when a new smudge appeared on the horizon. They would tell him, and he would make a note, not only of the location but of the landscapes, the ports and villages visible from the sea. Populations. Temples. Kings and the gods who favored them. He studied the maps, marking the places he knew to be treacherous from tales that Dictys had told them around the dinner table, and adding to it the knowledge of the men, each of whom had far more experience than he. Occasionally, when the chance occurred, he cast a net from the side of the boat and gathered fish for his men.

"All those muscles to gut a fish," one man said as Perseus took his knife to the belly of a palamida that he had caught in his net. The feel of the blade against the scales was a tender reminder of home. "Perhaps Athena would prefer to bestow her patronage on one of us instead."

"Perhaps I can see how well the skill of gutting transfers to a man?" Perseus replied, lifting his knife out of the fish. "Would you be volunteering for the post?" Laughter rippled through the men. After they ate, they talked about wives and families and women who were not their wives but by whom their families had been extended.

The night Perseus's second sibling paid him a visit, he had been feeling the pull of Seriphos stronger than ever before. The lack of cicadas or children shouting created an unease that he found impossible to displace, while the men's laughter from the other side of the boat only added to his feeling of isolation. Through time, he had earned their respect and their friendship, but their bonds had, as yet, experienced no adversity. Their shared stories spanned a length of months, not years or decades. If he were to leave that night, there would be no gaping hole in their lives, perhaps just a moderate hint of dolefulness for an hour or so. That night, the homesickness had struck painfully within his gut, the enormity and absurdity of what he had undertaken swilling through him like the sour drinks in which he wished to drown his sorrows.

He had removed himself from the crew and was alone in his quarters, a full goblet of wine resting on the table. Since boarding the boat, he had barely drunk a sip, mindful to keep his wits sharp for the journey, but that evening the oppressive heat and burgeoning anguish had driven him to pour himself a fresher taste. One sip had been enough though, and now his drink waited unattended, like all the other chores he had set for himself that night.

They had traveled far less that day than he had hoped. For the first time on his voyage, the winds had dropped, and the men were forced to use more and more of their own strength to keep them on course and drive them forward. With it came once again the realization that even with Pallas Athena on his side, the journey was not an easy one. Pursing his lips, he stared at his reflection. His hair had turned blonder from the salt and sun, his shoulders broader from the training, and the stubble that adorned his cheeks was now more akin to that of a man than a child. Pushing himself out of his seat, he passed his table and removed the mirrored item from the wall. This was it, Athena's gift. His single weapon against Medusa. A shield, polished to a perfect mirror.

"This way, you may see where the Gorgon sleeps, without risking her looking at you directly," Athena had told him.

"I am to kill her in her sleep?" Perseus questioned. "Is that not unsporting?"

"She is a monster, brother, not some deer you have stalked in the forest. You will kill her however you can, but I would not risk a time when her eyes are open."

Nodding as he listened, he brushed his hand over the polished silver, hoping that, somehow, the answers lay hidden beneath its surface. That night, he repeated the same circular strokes.

With a heavy groan, Perseus hung the shield back on the wall, abandoned his quarters, and headed for the deck.

The heat of the night was just as oppressive in the open, with no gentle breeze or rushing billow of the sails to cool him. He considered jumping overboard, plunging himself into the cool water for just a moment of relief. After all, low winds had to be good for something, and he was a strong swimmer. At this current rate of motion, he would be able to hold his pace with the boat for a short while at least.

"Not a good idea." A voice caused him to jump. "There are only so many times Poseidon will save you from the water. Particularly if you do something as stupid as jump."

His hair was knotted in tight curls, which, despite only moonlight above them, shined like the midday sun. In his hand, he held a staff of twisted snakes and wings. Around his ankles, he wore leather sandals adorned with wings so white they could have been made from fresh snow.

"Hermes?" Perseus found himself breathless in the presence of another sibling. Another god. He stared at the fluttering sandals, then at the caduceus in his hand before remembering his place and dropping to his knees. "You honor me with your visit."

The god's eyes twinkled. With a strong flap of the wings, he perched himself on the guardrail of the ship. "I suspect I do, yes." He grinned. "Well, brother, you are quite the talk up on Olympus. Quite the talk."

"I am?" Perseus spoke from the ground. In the mere moments he had known his sibling, he had come to suspect that Hermes was not the type who would tell a kneeling man to rise. His options, therefore, were to rise without waiting to be asked—and risk his half brother's wrath—or risk his knees growing numb on the splintered wood of the deck. After brief contemplation, he chose the former and slowly levered himself to standing.

Offering no rebuke, Hermes made no attempt to hide his intrigue as he surveyed Perseus in unnerving detail, scanning up and down his body; his chin nodded slightly, his lips parting in a grin. "You are becoming quite the hero, aren't you?"

His grin widened further still. The expression was far from the wry smile of his sister; it was an expression that suggested fun and frivolity. Yet somehow, it still managed to show the same level of concealment and pensiveness that Athena's had. Realizing he had not replied, and yet still unsure of what to say, Perseus opened his mouth to speak. Hermes's laugh stopped him.

"Don't worry. I'm not here to put any pressure on you. That's the role of the others. Actually, I came to offer a little bit of assistance. I saw that Athena gave you the shield. Sensible thinking. Now tell me, how do you suppose you will remove the monster's head from her neck?"

"How?" Perseus asked, puzzled. "With a sword. I have with me a xiphos that—"

"A xiphos?" Hermes's eyebrow slanted upward. "I feared as much. And tell me: If you do manage to remove the head with this mortal weapon, how then do you suppose you will carry it from her cave and back to Seriphos without turning yourself and your crew to stone?"

The moisture was rapidly drying from Perseus's mouth. Whether the questions were asked in good nature or as a trick was irrelevant. It was yet another aspect of the voyage for which he was ill prepared. Reading his face, Hermes lifted his hand and placed it on Perseus's shoulder. "Do not fear, brother; we are family. I am here to help you. You think Athena is the only one who can bestow gifts and patronize her heroes?" Despite the assurances, Perseus felt the knots in his stomach grow tighter, not looser. "Tell me, brother," Hermes continued. "Have you heard of the Graeae?"

TWENTY-FOUR

HIS MEN CHANGED THE SHIP'S COURSE WITHOUT A SINGLE question. There was no point waiting until the morning; time on the wrong path may have proved unsalvageable, so with the god still aboard, Perseus ordered his men to adjust accordingly.

"It will be a nice test for you," Hermes had said, apparently oblivious to Perseus's discomfort in his presence. "This little trip to the Gray Sisters may prove the making of you." While feigning the act of a hero among men was something Perseus felt he had mastered in these last months at sea, feigning heroism in front of a god was not something at which he was skilled. Greater muscles or not, his insides continued to twist and writhe.

"With the gods' blessings, the journey there will be swift," he replied.

"You are in a hurry, aren't you?"

"I am. I have to be. My, my..." Perseus considered mentioning his mother's name, only to close his mouth and keep the thought to himself. Hermes would already know of the event that had led him here, yet he had not discussed the matter with his crew and had no mind to do so. In their minds, he was another hero hungry for fame and glory, just with a slightly more impressive lineage.

His heart throbbed at the thought of this journey to the Graeae. Another task meant more time away from Seriphos, which in turn meant leaving his mother even longer in the hands of Polydectes. How long would it be before Polydectes announced Perseus as dead and took Danaë as his wife anyway? A man like him did not need evidence of a matter if it served a better outcome for him.

"You have the gods on your side." Hermes broke the silence. "You will be fine." He ran a finger along his caduceus. His whole hand glittered with the reflection. "Their island is close to Hades. You have not been that way before, I assume?"

"It is a journey I assumed I would make only once," Perseus replied. Goose bumps spread across his forearms at the thought of the underworld.

"But you are a hero, and you will do what must be done." There was no question at the end of his sentence. Perseus drew in a long even breath as he considered what awaited him.

"I will do what I must." He repeated his brother's words. "I will kill the Graeae for these items if I must."

"Kill them?" Hermes's eyes and mouth opened wide in horror, although a smile still flickered in the corner of his eyes. "They are old ladies, brother. Monstrous old ladies, but still. They will struggle to do you much harm with only one tooth and one eye among the three of them. Even we gods have principles, you know. No, they will give the items to you. They may need a little persuasion, however."

"Persuasion? How?"

"The method is of your design, brother. But don't worry, I will see you again after you are done." The god rested a hand on Perseus's shoulder as if he had been ever present in his life.

With that, the conversation drew to a close. Hermes cast his eye out to sea before turning back to Perseus one last time.

"Good luck, brother," he said again and let his winged sandals carry him toward the stars.

Despite their lack of complaint, Perseus watched as the men grew more and more agitated during their days traveling toward the underworld. Bickering broke out, only slightly, and possibly no more than it would have done anyway, but now, on this particular pathway, it had all grown more acute to Perseus. The scenery had changed. The lush green of the islands was replaced by more cragged, arid landscapes from which dust clouds rose above the earth in great plumes, obscuring the sun and plunging them into a false night. When it was not dust, it was clouds that blanketed the sky. Rainstorms of hail and sleet constantly stole the sun. His father's presence was evident in the forks of lightning that rattled across the sky, illuminating the perilous sea on which they sailed. Sometimes he wondered if they were signs of a father's compassion, each bolt warning him to turn back and go home defeated. He knew the reality though. He would return to Seriphos a hero or not at all.

The daily sparring continued, and with as many men as could be freed from their chores, yet the joy had lessened. The thought finally sank into him that he was not doing this to humor himself or to boost his ego. He was doing this to survive. Fighting was not the only part of his life in which the joy had lessened.

Food—which before the men had eaten freely with little concern for running short—Perseus was now forced to ration. The Goddess had provided them with all they would need to reach the Gorgons—not to mention the excess from Clymene—but their detour meant that they were likely to fall short by several days, if not longer. He cast his net more often, although the rougher waters gave little fish, and what they did catch tasted bitter, as if the flesh of their haul had been tainted with the grime and dust that now surrounded their existence.

Half a moon had passed since Hermes's visit when a knock on the door woke Perseus from his slumber. It had been a restless night, full of dreams of three-headed monsters holding his mother and his men hostage. He had tried to save them, only to fail time and time again. Sitting on thrones of stone, the gods had watched on, laughing, while Perseus struggled even to lift a spear. When he woke, sweat had drenched his skin, leaving dark marks on the bedsheets.

"Perseus, my lord." It was one of the Spartans. "The island is in view. We have reached the Graeae."

It looked to him more akin to a large rock than an island. Dusk was settling, casting the clouds in hues of crimson, as Perseus and two of his men rowed to land in the small wooden dingy, carrying with them a cloth satchel of oranges, preserved with salt, which Clymene had given to him. Persuasion came in many forms.

"One of you wait with the boat," Perseus told the two men. "The other, take a walk and see if there is anything on this island we can use. The women must find food somehow; see if there are any birds we can trap or places where fish seem to gather."

Nodding, and without a word exchanged to allocate the responsibilities, one of the men took off around the edge of the island, while the other hoisted the rope from inside the boat and secured it to a nearby rock. Perseus already knew in which direction he would head.

From their position, the island appeared so flat it would disappear during high tide. Only one area was raised higher than the rest of it. In the rock face was a dark shadow, a thin slit from which no light was emitted. A cave. Skirting along the coastline, Perseus gave himself a moment to feel his feet on firm ground. The rocks were black and porous, the air tinged with an ashy scent that reinforced in him the feeling of death that had been lingering in his thoughts since the journey began. Pushing them to the back of his mind, he started his ascent to the cave.

It was a pleasing realization to learn that his newly formed muscles worked as well on land as they did on the sea, and he scaled the height as easily as any man would take to a ladder. With one glance over his shoulder and to his boat, which rocked softly in the waves, he stepped into the shadows and the home of the Graeae. Voices echoed around him, the sounds reverberating off the walls.

"Tell us. Deino, tell us who it is."

"You must be able to see him now. He is in the cave now, is he not?"

"How do you know it is a man?"

"Oi, who is on my toe?"

Perseus shook his head, trying to find sense in the speech.

"How can you *not* tell it's a man? Can you not smell the musk, the meat?"

"Women have meat too. We were meaty once. I long for a good bit of meat between my jaws."

"I long for you to choke on a bit of meat."

Hissing and squealing interrupted the verbiage that came from every angle.

"Deino, give me the eye. Pemphredo, is that your hand in my ear? Get it off. Get it off."

"Why would my hand be in your ear? Deino, why are you staying silent? Curse you, sister. What do you see?"

A voice came through louder than the others. Less uncertainty in it. "I'm staying silent because I'm trying to hear over you two and all the racket you are making," it said. "Give me a moment."

"We already gave you a moment."

"You've been hogging it for—"

He could bear it no longer. Clearing his throat, he cast his voice out into the darkness in front of him. "I am Perseus, son of Zeus. I seek an audience with the Graeae."

A shrieking cackle rose out from within the cave.

"Son of Zeus! Deino, give me the eye. Give me the eye!"

In a flash, clawlike fingers grasped around his wrists and yanked him further into the cave.

"I've got him. I've got him!"

TWENTY-FIVE

THE MEAGER LIGHT FROM THE ENTRANCE WAS BARELY VISIBLE by the time Perseus regained his footing.

"Get off me!" He fought the instinct to reach for his sword. Instead, he lashed out with his feet and arms. A loud yelp reverberated through the air. He jerked his elbow, sending one of the creatures at the end of his arm onto the ground. A second later, and all three were back on him like rabid dogs, nipping at his heels.

"I am Perseus. Son of—"

"Son of Zeus, we heard you."

"It's our eyes that have gone, not our ears."

"Must be a half-mortal. Stupid like a mortal."

"He's definitely human. He smells like a human. Smell him, Eyno. And where is the eye?" Something damp and cold pressed up against his armpit. Something else prodded around his stomach. He recoiled further into the cave. The darkness was absolute. Each moment, he was twisted around, again and again, until all sense of direction was lost.

"I have come to seek an audience with you!" His rise in volume did little to deter them. He grasped at his sword, partially to comfort himself, partially to assure himself it wasn't ripped from him by one of their nimble fingers. Perseus's mind raced. Why did Hermes not warn him of this? With a shake of his head, he redirected his annoyance. It was his own stupidity. What sort of hero entered a cave without a torch to illuminate his way? And at dusk of all times. The easiest thing would be to abandon the task for that day. He would have to find his way out of the cave and back to the ship. Then he would come back at daybreak with a torch to guide his way. And maybe one or two men to spread the groping between.

With no idea which direction would take him further into the cave and which nearer the mouth, Perseus took a great step forward. His heart leaped as a glimmer of light flickered in the distance. With haste, he lunged toward it, surefooted against the uneven ground. The glory was short-lived. As he approached the source of the light, his stomach sank. Rather than finding himself at the entrance of the cave as he had hoped for, he found himself at the edge of a small fire, barely a flame among the embers. He cursed himself yet again. How was it possible that an island so small could be home to such a labyrinth of caves? Fish bones and animal carcasses littered the floor around the fire, and a dank stench of urine rose from the ground. Broken pots with jagged edges piled up against the wall, while full pots—the contents of which Perseus wished not to know— sat overflowing around the makeshift hearth. For a second, he was momentarily grateful for the lack of light.

"Where are you going?" The gabbling started again. "That's not the way out."

"Maybe he wants to stay."

"Tell us, son of Zeus, what can we do for you?"

Hunched over, they followed him, scuttling like spiders. With another ambush only seconds away, Perseus drew his sword out and swept an arc in front of him, unconvinced that any of the hags could even see the threatening gesture.

"Will you be quiet?"

The women squealed and scurried into a corner. Huddled into one another, they wheezed and panted. "What did we do?"

"We only asked a question."

"We only wanted to see."

"I have not seen him! Where is the eye? Give me the eye, or I swear this tooth in my mouth will soon be embedded in your rear end."

The skin on their cheeks sagged inward into the hollows of their mouths. Their frail bodies twisted at angles, while sores, swollen in welts and oozing pus, covered their skin. In the dimness, he saw something exchange hands. Round and glistening, their single eye.

Swallowing down the nausea that struck again and again, Perseus scanned his surroundings. If the gods were kind, his sight might fall on the very items he needed. He could carry off the whole contents of the cave and be done with these women before another word was exchanged. Yet all he could see within the detritus was yet more squalor. The stench rolled out in waves. With his sword still out, he considered his next action. Hermes had cautioned him to be gentle, but how to get their attention without forcing them? Girding himself with all the power of his father, he attempted yet again to gain their attention and help.

"My name is Perseus, son of Zeus, and I have been sent by the God—"

"He does like talking about gods, doesn't he?"

"Maybe it's his mind that's gone. Maybe that's why he repeats himself so much. Let me see him. I still haven't seen him."

He had not finished a single sentence. Was it too much to ask? "You creatures are intolerable."

Loud cackles echoed off the walls of the cave.

"Ooo."

"The god's son knows some big words."

"Very big words."

"I don't think I'm intolerable. Do you think I'm intolerable, sisters?"

His patience had frayed to its limit. Perseus leaped over the fire, grabbed the wrist of the one who had just spoken, and dragged her away from her sisters. In the glimmers of the embers, he held his sword to her throat. Her translucent skin yielded under the pressure of the sword, causing a single bead of blood to appear on the blade.

"If you will not listen to me by choice, so be it. But you will listen to me. I have been sent by Hermes. I have been favored by Athena, the Goddess of Wisdom and War. You have items that I require to fulfill my destiny to rid the world of the Gorgon Medusa. You will speak to me your truths, or you will understand the power of my wrath."

His final words resonated around the walls, causing icy chills to shift through the air. Silence followed. His own heart drummed as he awaited their reply. He was a born hero, he reminded himself. Now they could hear it too. The body tensed in his arms. A moment later, it erupted into laughter.

"Ooo, he's got me. Sisters, he's got me!"

"Give me the eye. I want to see."

"He's ever so muscly." Her hands roamed up his arms, squeezing and pinching him. "Take me captive, Perseus, son of Zeus. Hold poor Eyno prisoner. Tie me up and whip me!"

The old woman's laugh barked out again. Soon, the other two were on him as well.

"No, take me, take me. She can barely bend her knees without falling over."

"Perhaps that's what he likes. I'd happily drop onto my knees for you, Perseus. There's an advantage to having no teeth, you know." A wet, sucking noise slapped from her lips. Perseus gagged, fearing he could take no more of their grotesque innuendo, and then, in the most revolting of acts, the one he now knew to be Eyno began to run her hands over the fabric covering her chest, pressing herself to him and emitting low guttural moans.

"We don't get many men here. Stay a little while."

"We're old, but we still have needs."

"No more," Perseus said and threw Eyno to her sisters in disgust. The laughing rose in dissonance.

"Look at his face! What a picture. I bet he's never even seen a naked woman."

"Let me see. Let me see! I need the eye."

"You've already seen him. Let me have a chance. Let me have my turn."

Still shuddering, he watched as the eye exchanged hands in quick succession. Glistening and wet, it rolled off and onto the palms of their hands before disappearing into one of their sunken sockets with a pop.

"Oh, the poor boy." The Graeae continued their repulsive lament. "He's only a lad."

"I want another look. What have you done to him now?"

"You're hogging it. Stop hogging it!"

It was an impulsive decision rather than a carefully considered one. Whose hand it was in, he could not tell. But the moment he saw it drop out from a socket and onto a palm, ready for exchange, Perseus leaped across the space and snatched it up in his hand. Screams reverberated around the cave.

"What are you doing? What are you doing? Pemphredo, was that you? Stop it. Stop it!"

"It's him. It's him!"

Perseus squeezed the item in his grasp. The graying flesh yielded and squelched a little between his fingers. An agonizing scream splintered the dark.

"You!" The old women doubled over in pain, clutching and clawing at their eye sockets as though he were digging his nails directly into their skulls. Anticipating their reactions, he squeezed the eyeball a little harder.

"Stop it! Stop! Have mercy on us!" Their words were broken by whimpers, like the dogs in Seriphos beaten within an inch of their lives for daring to steal a bone. Perseus had never been one of those to hurl stones at dogs, other than when they bared their teeth at him, but at that moment, the sisters had given him very little choice.

"I have your eye." Perseus's voice resonated with the power of his heritage. "I have it, and I will crush it between my fingers if you do not give me what I need."

"No!" They were on their knees, begging and pleading, barely able to stand from the agony that he had caused them with just a flex of his fingers.

"I have been sent by Hermes himself to retrieve the items I need to succeed in my quest."

One of the women crawled forward on the ground.

"Return the eye. Return the eye, oh merciful one, and we will give you what you need."

"You will give me what I need first, and then I will return the eye."

"How can we see, you fool?" The pleading voice turned bitter and venomous. "You would have us crawl on the ground, all three of us blind? We could break a limb with a trip or plummet to our death while we search."

"If you are worried about tripping, you should take better care of your home. You are in a cave with no risk of falls from what I can tell. Neither of your risks seems likely to me." Perseus was beginning to find his stride. His shoulders extended back as he spoke. "And don't worry. My reflexes are good. I will catch you if need be. Now tell me where to find the items I require, and I will be on my way."

Muttering replaced the cries as he released the pressure on the eye. Their scowls, although he would have thought it not possible, deepened into such a web of ravines that it was almost impossible to tell where an eye or mouth or nose might have even been. Just folds of skin, no flesh or muscle, thinner than dried grasses at the end of summer.

"Fine," one said finally, the bitterness in her voice as tangible as the stench that continued to pervade them all. "You will find what you want on the west side of the cave. By the entrance. It is back the way you came."

Perseus's eyes flitted. The light had helped a little, but should he get turned around again in the dark, he would have no way to regain his bearings.

"You can lead the way," he said.

The now familiar cackle broke into the air. "How? We cannot see, you fool. Did you not listen a minute ago? What you have in muscles you have lost in brain cells."

Uncertainty gnawed at Perseus. It could easily be a trick. Another ploy to overthrow him once one of them was returned the power of sight. Yet, he would be prepared this time. He pulled out his dagger, strode across the cave, and grasped the nearest hag by the arm. A squeal like that of a pig before its throat is slit shot through the air as he yanked the old woman toward him. He thrust the eye into her palm while pointing the tip of his blade beneath the woman's rib.

"Any trickery and I will plunge this into your flesh. You have worn my patience down." A sound of suction followed as she replaced the eyeball into her left socket. "Now move," he said.

With her spine curved like a hook, she was barely hip height to him as she dragged her feet in front of Perseus. Every few shuffles, she would cast her gaze over her shoulder, and in turn Perseus jabbed the blade into the spindly lines of her ribs until, with a yelp or squeal of pain, she continued on. The remaining two Graeae wailed in the corner. Their incongruous cries provided a suitably dissonant backdrop to the absurdity of the situation. In Seriphos, even the craziest of old women were treated with some degree of respect. He shuddered to think what his mother would think at the sight of him now.

"Here. On the left. In that hole. You will need to lift them out." The Graeae stopped and pointed to a fissure in the rocks. She had brought him close to the mouth of the cave, although he had yet to see whether there was any truth in whether the items would be found there. He would not put it past them to lead him to a cranny full of scorpions in the hopes that they would sting him to an agonizing death.

"You will retrieve them," Perseus said.

"Me? Do you not see how old I am? How can I lift such items?"

"I do not care how you do it. Just do it." He pressed the blade deeper into her skin. His stomach lurched as he felt the skin yield a little bit. *Can something so withered bleed?* he wondered. And what color would it even be? Surely nothing so gray could bleed red like a man. He cast the thoughts of blood aside as, with grousing words beneath her breath, the old woman reached her hand into the crevice and pulled out the hilt of a sword. Even in the darkness, the metal glinted.

"Here," she said. "Do you believe me now? This is as much as I can hold it. Take it if you want it. I'll be damned if I'm going to hold it here for you until my arms pop out of their sockets."

Seeing no sign of a trap, Perseus took the hilt from the hag and pulled the length of the sword out into the open. It was unlike any material he had ever held. No blacksmith on Seriphos had forged from this metal, of that he was sure.

"It is made from adamant," the Graeae said as if reading his thoughts. "Belonged to Zeus himself."

Perseus turned the blade over in his hands, hefting it to gauge its weight. It was perfectly balanced as if it had been made solely for him.

"Where did you get such an item?" he asked.

The single eye of the withering woman narrowed. "Do you tell me all your secrets? No, you do not. You have it now. Be happy with that."

In the pale light of the cave, his reflection glimmered in the sword.

"What about the Kibis?" The voice of the second Graeae echoed from the back of the cave. "He'll need the Kibis, won't he?"

"Yes, yes, he'll need it. Give it to him, Deino. Give it to him."

"I'm getting there. You try moving with a dagger digging into your ribs."

"The Kibis?" Perseus questioned. Deino's eye rolled backward in a swooping circle of derision.

"Here." This time, she made no qualms about reaching into the crevice, and from it, she pulled out a brown sack, similar in size to the one in which Perseus had brought them the preserved oranges. Not that he planned on leaving it with them now.

"It's for the head." One of the others called again. "When you cut off the head, you must put it in here."

Taking the item from her, he squinted. The material felt strong but light, yet at its size, it would fail to hold whole even one of the serpents, let alone the entire head of Medusa.

"Put the sword in it." Deino read his doubt. "You don't believe me. Put the sword in it."

Hesitating for only a moment, Perseus opened the laced top of the bag, certain it would struggle to hold even a fraction of the blade. Yet, as he gently lowered the sword down the cloth of the bag, it changed shape, expanding and shrinking as it needed to accommodate the item within.

"The Gorgon's head will fit perfectly within it, as will any other treasure you hold," Deino told him. Perseus turned the bag around in his hand. The lightness of it was beyond belief.

"This is the work of the gods?" he said, although the obviousness of his words felt foolish as they left his lips.

"It is," the Graeae said, and for the first time since his arrival in the cave, she locked the single eye squarely on his. "Now you've got what you want," she spat. "Get out of here."

TWENTY-SIX

DAYS TURNED INTO WEEKS. THE GRAY SEAS CAUSED THEM TO lose their way and turn back on themselves, again and again. Thick clouds shrouded the stars at night, stealing their source of navigation. During the day, only a dusky glow of sunlight could help guide them on their way. Then one day, it all lifted.

The relief that the crew felt at a cerulean sky was not shared by their captain. Perseus could feel the event looming on the horizon, a static hum that buzzed in the air around him, warning him of his impending doom. Every day spent at sea was a day closer to meeting the Gorgon.

That night, the stars glinted in the clear sky. The sea rippled, an inky pool around the ship. He knew it would not be long, just like he knew that one of his siblings would appear to him one last time before he reached his fate. In his heart, he had hoped for Athena; her wisdom and knowledge of battle were what he needed to encourage him. But the color that glinted in the sky was gold, not gray.

"I hear you gave the Graeae a scare." Hermes perched himself on the edge of the stern with a casual arrogance Perseus had grown to associate with him.

"Me? I think it was the other way around. For blind old women, they can move quickly."

"Oh, I know. But you succeeded in your first task. You must be feeling just a little bit confident." Perseus dwelled on the thought for a moment. It was luck rather than judgment that had helped him succeed with the Graeae without bloodshed, and he was not naive enough to think otherwise.

"So," Hermes said, ending the moment of contemplation. "With that little job over and done, are you prepared for what will come next?"

"For the Gorgons, can anyone be prepared?"

"Gorgon," Hermes said, emphasizing the singularity of the word.

"Gorgon? There will only be one? How do you know?" It had been a thought playing on his mind since he had first left Seriphos, although he had refused to voice his concern, even to his men on the ship. Sometimes, when he caught their eyes, he swore they were having the same thought. He was to bring Polydectes the head of Medusa, but she was only one Gorgon. There was a distinct possibility that he would never even make it to their queen. If they were anything like the Graeae, the three may well be bonded at the hip.

"The sisters took flight." Hermes once again demonstrated his irritating ability to voice Perseus's thoughts before he had spoken them. "Three weeks have passed since they left the island. If my information is correct, they are terrorizing ships around the Diapontia."

"And when will they be back?"

"Who can tell? I'm sure if the gods are on your side, you should get ample time. How long does it take to sneak into a cave and decapitate a priestess?" He winked as he spoke.

"A priestess?"

"A priestess?" Hermes's head shook a little. "What a strange choice of word. Forgive me. Clearly, I have gone too long without a woman's touch if I have priestesses on my mind. As I was saying, it will not take long to behead one single beast, I am sure."

Perseus twisted his lips, not sure how to respond. Leaning over, Hermes began to unbuckle the straps of his sandals.

"The Gorgon, she is born from the sea, is she not?"

Hermes's eyes narrowed. "Monsters of the sea. Is that what they say? And why not? It is as good a story as any."

"I am grateful that I will not have to tackle her in the water." A hint of fear pulsed through Perseus. "I won't, will I?"

Hermes laughed. "I sincerely doubt it, brother. I sincerely doubt it. Now," he said, the twinkle firmly back in his eye. "How about one last gift? Then I'll let you be on your way."

Medusa had taken advantage of the quiet and partaken in a few days of pruning. Century after century, the figures stacked up, one after another after another. Many were forced from statue to pebble at the will of the gods; the sun's heat made stone turn brittle, ice and snow weakened it further still, and a good storm could see tens of figures turned into dust with just a few days of solid rain and wind. Others were victims of Stheno and Euryale's boredom during the quiet years.

Like cats who continued to play and decimate a dead mouse's carcass, her sisters would take pleasure in the stone effigies that decorated their garden. Sometimes they would use their talons to scrape crude drawings into the stone bodies. Other times, they would make use of the hundreds of discarded weapons that were dropped in the spray as those with more sense ran back to their ships only moments after setting foot on the stony shore. They never made it, though. The ones who ran were always Euryale's favorites. She would swoop and dive back and forth, taunting them for as long as possible before finally turning them to stone.

Many of the statues in the garden were without arms, or heads, or whatever else the sisters swung the blades at when the fancy took them. At least headless meant Medusa no longer felt the weight of their hollow gazes; all the fear a man could ever know was directed toward her, the scent of their fear still present after all these years. Maybe that was in her head, she thought more than once. The smells were merely appropriations, like the screams that kept her up most nights.

Ridding herself of the statues was never easy. Her hatred and pity for the men who had come to kill her were as indivisible as those same emotions she felt for her sisters. So, she took her time, disposing of them one by one.

The sounds of waves breaking into foam drifted to her ears as she reached her hand up to one of the statues. Gingerly, she touched the place where his hair would once have flowed. A second later, she grabbed him around the throat and hoisted him up. One by one, she dragged them to the edge of the cliff and flung them off the side, watching as their human form shattered into pieces.

Her work was slow. The cool air made her snakes sluggish and irritable. They fought among themselves, although, often, she ended up the victim of their aggression. Their manner reminded her of siblings—normal human siblings—who bickered and quarreled only to cry out in distress should they have to be parted. Not that the snakes could be parted, of course. Thoughts of her siblings led to thoughts of her parents, which slowed her work even more. They would have been in the underworld for millennia now, their names forgotten by every living person on earth. Assuming they had had a burial, of course. It was a thought that tormented her often. Another act at which she had failed.

Her distracted mind meant she had failed to drag even half of the statues to the edge of the cliff by the time the sun was on its downward arc. With her sisters gone, no doubt she would have more time tomorrow to finish the rest. Gazing at the sea, she tilted her head, and for the first time that day, she noticed the change in the wind. Static filled the air, an invisible charge that swarmed around her in dizzying currents. Her snakes could feel it too. They quietened, pressing their bodies against her as if they were preparing for a fight. She knew what it was. She could smell it in the air just the same as they could. Another hero was on the way.

He checked the strap on the shield for the third time and then the fourth. He still wasn't familiar with the nuances of shields; before this time, he had never had the need, and the only ones he had held on Seriphos had been the makeshift toys of boys playing with wooden swords. Even sparring on the ship, he had quickly abandoned the use of one, relying instead on his nimble feet to dodge his opponent's blade. But inexperienced or not, he wasn't stupid. He knew Athena would not have given him such a gift without a reason, and until this point, he had put absolute faith in his sister. Yet, that afternoon, with the island growing ever larger on the horizon, he felt less than fully assured by the armor's lightness. The thinness of the metal now seemed impractical, like it could be pierced by a single snakebite, let alone the dozens he was soon to encounter. Hopefully, he would not get close enough for them to strike. And at least she would not hear him coming. Hermes's sandals should see to that. With the sword too, he couldn't help but think that the only weak link in his armory supplied by the gods to kill Medusa was him.

With the ship anchored in the bay, Perseus readied the small rowing boat for himself. Many of his men had volunteered to come with him. He suspected they all would, even without the duress of a direct order, but he chose to make the journey on his own. Better that only one life be lost. His strength and skill now surpassed those of even the best of his crew. If he was unable to succeed in the mission, it was impossible to imagine that one of his men would. Better that they had their sails up and ready to depart before the sisters returned and cast them all in stone for his stupidity.

"If I succeed, I will return before the first rays of sunrise," he told them before he left. "You will see my boat leaving from the shore. If I am not within your sight before the sun breaks the horizon, go. Do not wait. Do not, under any circumstances, follow me to the island. Leave. Sail fast. You will have the gods on your side and the wind at your back. When you reach land, build an altar to the gods in my name. To my father. My siblings. If I do not succeed in my task, it will be the fault of my inadequacies, not theirs. You will be free men. By Athena's will, sell this boat and split the proceeds among you. It will see you all rich men."

It would be a true test of their loyalty, Perseus considered, to see whether they were pleased to see him return or not.

They nodded and held his gaze. A few tentative smiles made their way to him. They were, he realized as he rowed his boat away from his men and toward his destiny, possibly the last smiles he would ever see.

———

Only one this time. She had seen him standing on the edge of the boat, addressing his crew. It was not uncommon. She had seen this before. Listened in enough times to know that they said the same things, some with a little more eloquence, and some with a lot more folly and crudity than others. They all spoke of glory. Of unimaginable riches and rewards that would be afforded them when they succeeded in bringing home her head. Many mentioned the women who would either fall at their feet or men who would be forced to their knees upon their return. Medusa always made sure that those were left to her sister's games where possible. The wise ones left messages for their families and friends. However, wisdom, she noticed, was not something lavishly bestowed on the neophyte heroes.

So, in the last few centuries, she had stopped listening to their speeches. She had heard enough. Heard the arrogance time and time again. The presumption and complacency with which they spoke about any murder—let alone her own—so easily caused anger to swell through her in waves. The weight of each of her murders, each death by her gaze, was heavier than any stone effigy she could have ever formed, yet some of these men viewed killing as a sport. Sometimes she wished they knew that as they stood there on their decks, spouting their words, it was not victory speeches that left their lips but eulogies.

A distant storm rumbled beyond the horizon. She would not have the advantage of her sisters tonight then. It was as she was turning away from the sea to begin her retreat to the caves that the snakes reared upward. They coiled over her skull with the energy of a summer morning. Their tongues flickered out of their mouths, tasting the air around them.

"What is it?" she said. She was still trying to sense the source of their discomfort when she caught the aroma that clung to the figure approaching her shore. Cold and metallic, but also fresh and fruity. It was not something she had experienced before, or at least not in a long time. Memories stirred in the deepest crevices of her mind. A tremor palpitated in her chest.

"They have sent me a god," she whispered. "They have sent me a god."

TWENTY-SEVEN

H E FOUND LITTLE COMFORT IN HIS NEW FORM OF TRANS-
port. This must be what it was like to be a god, he thought,
as he floated up from the shoreline. Thankfully, he had
rowed ashore and strapped on the sandals only after pulling the boat
up onto the beach. Otherwise, he would be arriving at the Gorgon
soaked to the skin in seawater. The sandals were not the most conve-
nient to manage; a little practice should probably have been advised.
They had their advantages; brambles and rocks proved no obstacle,
provided the distance he had to cover in each situation was no more
than a couple of feet. Every time he lifted up, the lack of ground
beneath his feet caused his stomach to lurch. Men were not, he
discovered, designed to fly. The plate around his chest made the top
of his body heavy, and more than once he toppled forward. With no
solid ground to help maintain his balance, he found himself flail-
ing in the air, flapping his arms like a fledgling. And like so many
fledglings, he was quickly grounded. It did not take him long to
abandon the sandals for the time being. The island was sizable, and
with his current pace of flying back and forth, he was unlikely even

to reach the Gorgon's lair by sunrise. Slipping them off, he buckled the straps around his waistband and continued inland. He would use the sandals when he was closer. After all, there was no chance she would be able to hear him yet.

His clumsy approach was deafening even over the storm that had followed him onto the shore. Thunder and lightning now antagonized the snakes. Every bolt seared heat through the air, causing them to recoil and hiss. The false hero was making good speed toward them now, heading up the path that led to the garden. For a while, she hoped he had changed his mind, fled back into the night from whence he came, as only the wisest or most cowardly ones did. Her hope was short-lived. None ever turned back now. Not unless they were running. Now it was just a case of waiting.

When he entered the garden, she heard the change in his gait. That in itself was not unusual. Even the most surefooted staggered and stumbled at the sight of their fate staring back at them through stony pupils. Stifled cries and muttered prayers would frequently reach her ears, though not from this one. Not the one with the scent of Olympus coursing through his veins. The scent of the Goddess.

She forgave herself for the delay in recognizing the scent exactly. It had been two millennia since she had inhaled the sweet aroma, and back then her senses had been far from the keen masterpieces they had become. Yet, now that she had realized it, it was impossible to shake the memories that came with this stranger's arrival. Athena's scent was all over him.

As he wove his way through the statues, Medusa had no doubt that whoever this boy was, he was one of the Goddess's heroes. Or at least had been at some time. It was more likely that he had fallen out of favor with the Goddess of Wisdom. That had to be it, for why else would she have sent him to the island if not for him to meet his end? Another youth for whom she no longer had a use. For a moment, Medusa closed her eyes and pondered what act he could have done to irk the Goddess in such a manner, but it did not matter. She would try to make his death swift at least. It was the same grace she offered to all the men who set foot on her island. It was only after finishing her contemplation of these facts that Medusa became aware that the hero's steps had altered. They no longer reverberated through the ground the way the footsteps of a man normally did. Instead, what she heard was a fluttering.

"Sisters?" She voiced her thoughts aloud only to shake them away the instant they had formed. Her sisters did not flutter. Their great wings beat the air with the delicacy of pelicans coming in to land. This was more like a hummingbird. A finch, perhaps. Yet it was like none she had ever heard before. Her skin prickled, and her shoulders shrank back. Her snakes hissed into the dark, rapid, irate hissing in all directions. Many, many years had passed since she last felt such a sensation. Fear. She was afraid.

Slowly, she edged backward into one of the many crevices of the cave and out of sight. A moment later, and he too was standing in her lair.

With her heart trembling, Medusa waited for the boy to make his move. Any men who had previously been allowed to get this far charged on, confident that having made it through the garden, their success was guaranteed. But not this one. For all the ichor of the gods running through his veins, she could feel the nerves clouding his mind.

"Who are you?" Medusa said. "Why did the Goddess send you?"

Her snakes were poised. The sensation of terror had gone as

quickly as it had come. It was not fear of this man, she realized, just memories of the Goddess that caused her body to react so. He was just a man, a boy, like all the others she had been forced to kill. Now that he was securely past the mouth of the cave, his breath created a warm fog that drifted inward to the cool of the shadows. She cursed herself for allowing him to get this far. Now she would have to drag his effigy out into the garden before ridding herself of it that way. Extra work. Extra time spent looking into those cold stone eyes.

"I know you are here. You should turn back," she called into the darkness. "You have been sent on a fool's errand. No man escapes here, no matter who sent him." The same near-silent buzzing continued, although she heard the air tighten in his lungs. Medusa tried again. "Go. While you still have the chance. Do you hear me? You do not want to face me, boy. Run, while you still can."

Another pause. An intake of breath perceptible only to her. A quiver in the air before even the first word had formed on his lips. She waited for the bold statements. The declaration of heroism. A list of all his conquests. A rhetoric of the reasons that he would be the first to succeed where all others had failed.

She planned to reveal herself, to turn him the moment those words began, but the words he spoke were not as expected.

"Who are you?" he said.

The words sounded foolish and childish as they spilled from his mouth. He had words he should have said, words he had recited in his head. Strong words, praising the gods. Giving thanks to his father and siblings. Perhaps even shouting their names as he slipped the sword across the beast's throat. But that was what he had expected. A beast. Guttural growls and spitting hisses. He expected the tongue of a serpent, not the tongue of a woman.

An explanation tried to form in his head; he must have stumbled upon another island. One where the Gorgons kept their prizes. Perhaps she was a woman held captive by the beasts. Perhaps she needed to be rescued and, as such, would become part of his reward. It was his turn to speak and ask the questions.

"Who are you?" Perseus asked again. "My name is Perseus. I have come from Seriphos."

"I am the one you seek," the voice replied.

"I have come for the Gorgon Medusa."

His words were met with a laugh that bounced off the walls of the cave, distorting the direction from which it came. "Tell me," she said. "What did you do to invoke such anger in the Goddess that she would send you to me? You must have riled her a great deal."

"Angered?"

"Athena, she sent you, did she not?" the voice pressed. "I can smell her on you."

Perseus was having difficulty focusing. His mind was muddled by the turn in the encounter.

"I am the son of Zeus. The Goddess Athena is my half sister. She sent me on my voyage with her blessing."

"Her blessing? Be careful. It is as likely to change as the wind."

A game was being played. He could feel it, and then he heard it. Subtle and low and as quiet as the hum of Hermes's wings. The flicker of tongues. The hissing of snakes.

"You are the Gorgon." His pulse surged at the knowledge that he had been so close to the monster all this time and not even realized the risk.

"Like I said. I am the one you seek."

With the speed of a true hero, Perseus whipped his sword out in front of him and turned in a circle. Laughter echoed as he swung blindly in the air.

"You should save your strength," the Gorgon said. "You will never get close enough to strike. My snakes will see to that."

"I do not believe you."

"Then try. I am over here."

A sound rang out. A stone, clinking against the floor. Perseus's eyes rushed in the direction where a small stone bounced along the ground, coming to rest a little way from his feet. It was a trap, no doubt, but he was unlikely to manage his task while rooted at the entrance of the cave. He stepped farther inside.

Perseus cast his eyes around him. The cavern was larger than the Graeae's had been, and light filtered in from various cracks and fissures, allowing him to see a little better. Several passageways wove off in different directions. In one of these, who knew which, hid the monster.

"If you are the Gorgon, then why not strike me down now? Why continue on with this foolish game if all you wish for is to kill me? I didn't know you liked to toy with your victims."

"I suspect you know very little of me at all." She spoke as a matter of fact. "Tell me, Perseus, son of Zeus, half sister to the Goddess of Wisdom. Did she tell you what befell a priestess to be worthy of this crown of serpents?"

"Priestess?" The same word used by Hermes. "You were a priest-ess for the Goddess?"

A short silence followed. His pulse became erratic. His sword remained poised, fingers twitching at the spare dagger at his side.

"Tell me, Perseus." The Gorgon Priestess spoke. "Are you a man of the world?"

He cleared his throat. "I am the captain of my ship. I have here voyaged from Seripho—"

"And on this voyage." She cut through his words before he had a chance to finish. "Your men—was their behavior fitting? Manly? Did they cast their power outward, lord it over the women at the docks who fluttered eyelashes at them?"

"My men are good men. Our journey has been long. We have not made port for many weeks."

"But when they did? They expressed their freedom, I suspect? How widely? Did they make claims? What about the women who didn't seek out their gazes? Were they left in peace or harangued and harassed for your men's gratification?"

"A man..." Perseus stepped forward, finally deducing the meaning of her riddles. "A man forced himself upon you?"

"A man?" She snorted. The sound of her derision riled the snakes, causing them to hiss with such venom that the hairs on the back of his neck stood on end. "You think a man would dare desecrate the temple of a god in such a manner? To defile anything sacred to one of the gods? Would one of your men?" This time, he knew there was no need to answer. No man in his right mind would ever consider such a thing.

"A god?" he whispered.

"Yes." The single word expelled in a bloom of air. "Yes. It was a god who forced himself upon me in such a manner that would make your innocent eyes look away in terror. It was a god who bloodied my body and broke my will. And it was another god, a goddess, who tore apart everything I had left. Your uncle and your sister took everything I had."

"Athena?"

She did not indulge him with a reply.

"Gods do not pay the price for their wrongdoings, Perseus. Mortals do. The gods, like the rich of the world, push their agendas onto those whose voices are not loud enough to speak for themselves. The women. The weak. The unwanted. And no one shouts for those who need it the most. Why would they? To shout for another is to risk losing something yourself. And man cannot see beyond the depth of his own reflection."

A cold breeze moved in from the sea, although Perseus paid it no heed. His head swam with the words of the Gorgon.

"The Goddess did this to you? Because of another god's actions upon you?"

"You do not believe me?" Her retort was fast, sharp. He shook his head, then wondered if there was any chance she should see.

"How do I not know of this? Why would people not know? Surely you must have told others." The story of his own conception through the golden rain was known far and wide, as was that of many a cursed soul who had angered the gods. If such a thing had happened to a priestess, it seemed impossible that he would not have heard.

Once again came the bitter laugh, although now within it, Perseus heard a sadness. An angry melancholy.

"Four people knew the actions of Poseidon and the Goddess. My parents, who both died under my gaze when I was unaware of its power, and my sisters, who were transformed into beasts more heinous than even me for the act of daring to question Athena's decision."

"No, it cannot be," Perseus voiced, although as he spoke the words, he knew the Gorgon's story to be true.

"You have gone quiet," she said after a moment. "I understand. There is nothing like the truth to silence men. And now I will be forced to kill again, as I have done a thousand times on this shore, for

I have no other option. My serpents, the Goddess, they will not have it any other way. Once, people came to me for help, for advice. Now they come to make me a murderer time and time again."

Outside the cave, the sound of the waves rose up as they crashed against the shore. Inside the cave, only the sound of the snakes remained. The tremble in his hand, Perseus noticed, had stopped, and when he stepped forward, his sword hung limply by his side. The hiss of the serpents was louder now. Less reverberation from their sound. She had not lied about her location, Perseus thought as he approached a narrow passageway. Coming to a halt, he pressed his back against the cold, damp wall. For a moment, his thoughts flitted away from Medusa and returned to their frequent residence, to his mother. Would there be someone in the palace of Polydectes who would stand up for her? She was a woman forced to conceive by a god. Forced out of her home into a life she did not want or deserve because of the will of others. Not for a second had he thought he would find a single similarity between the creature he had come to kill and the woman he had left to save, yet he worried if she spoke any more, he would find it impossible to complete his task. Moments had passed, and he realized that he had not yet replied to the Priestess. And yet, when his mouth opened, he could offer nothing more than an apology.

"I am sorry," he said.

TWENTY-EIGHT

S HE FELT LIKE A FOOL. WHAT HAD POSSESSED HER TO TALK TO this young man? It made no sense. Thousands of years, and she had never felt the need to unburden the knowledge of her creation onto any of the men who stormed onto her island. But this was different. He had come under the guidance of Athena, and if that was the case, it was her duty to remove the blindfold from his eyes. He needed to see the Goddess for who she was. Finally, she heard an intake of breath.

"I am sorry."

The words took a moment to strike her.

"I do not need your sympathies," she said. "I am well past the judgment of mortals."

"And yet you were a human once, so you must know that words can have meaning?"

She snorted a response, although his words had already taken a hold, embedding themselves within her. Of course, she remembered the power of words. She remembered all about promises and vows, and the effects when these were broken. She still recalled the eyes of all the women whose vows had been made ridiculous by their errant husbands. She remembered how her own feeble human frame had been ruined far more by the words of disdain from the Goddess than any physical act from Poseidon. She knew that true words from a man were more valuable than shallow gifts from a god. But this man, this boy? He was just another murderer come to claim a prize.

"I have a mother," the boy said, piercing the silence.

"Most men do." Her curt response was meant as humor, but the lack of reply she received caused her to regret her decision. She could hear him swallowing, his pulse stuttering. With a great deal more softness than she had used in centuries, she said, "Tell me."

The pause elongated between them, the mist his breath caused in the air now so close she could taste it. Heat radiated from his body. Was that the warmth of a demigod or merely of a man? It had been so long since she had spent any significant amount of time in the company of a person such as this that she no longer knew. *How would it feel to be embraced by such a warmth?* she wondered. Held close just for the sake of compassion. Her snakes hissed at her daydreaming. Of course, that could never be. She would never know the comfort of warm arms and human flesh again. "Your mother," she said, prompting him to continue. "Tell me about her."

He did not start immediately, and even when he did, there was a hesitancy to his tone, a stiltedness as the words left his lips.

"She raised me. There were other people too. I had a family, but my mother, she is…special. That sounds silly, I know. Every child must feel the same, but my mother is… She was chosen by Zeus for a reason. No better person could I have wished for in my life." A dull throb extended out from her chest, a reminiscence of the way she had felt about her father. "She is betrothed to a man," Perseus continued. "A powerful man. A king."

"And this displeases you?"

"He is vile." Perseus spat his words. "Hideous and rotten to the core."

Medusa listened on, pity swelling in her heart. The passageway she had slipped into felt longer than it had. She felt no risk in moving a little closer toward Perseus as he continued to talk. "This king, he has no shame. His eyes, they wandered across her like a prize. A goat for slaughtering. My mother, she is a strong woman. A brave woman. She has endured so much. Yet I wonder how much this man will test even her will. When I consider… When I…" His words drifted into his thoughts. It didn't matter. Medusa knew their meaning. She had felt them herself all those years.

"And you are here because of him?" she said.

"I promised him the head of the Gorgon as a wedding present."

"A bold present indeed. You know my gaze would turn any man who looked upon it to stone?"

"I do."

"So, your gift to him would be an eternal one?"

"I can but hope."

He waited for her reply. His warmth was waning, wicking into the air around him. Outside, the sun had set, and the rays of light that had diffused into the cave were fading fast. She was inches away from him; he knew that. Yet as long as he remained flush against the rock, he would be safe. Safety in the Gorgon's cave. Even he could see the irony, feeling safe in the home of a monster. It had been a mistake to tell her the reason for his visit. Now she knew his weakness. Perhaps this was always her play, lulling men into a feeling of safety before casting that final strike. In a heady daze, he realized his sword was completely lowered. He whipped it into the air.

"I would offer you my head. Gladly." Her words caught him by surprise. "But it cannot be. The Goddess will not let me die. My serpents, they will stop it. There is no way. I have tried. Believe me, child. I have tried."

"You have tried to end your life?" Perseus failed to hide the surprise in his voice.

"You think I would choose this? The gods wish to make me suffer for all eternity. That is the truth. As long as Zeus reigns upon Olympus and Athena holds his ear, I am destined for torment."

Perseus considered her words. His limbs had grown stiff. Motionless conversation was not something he had practiced in preparation for the event. Looking down at the mirrored surface of his shield, he noted the deep creases furrowed in his brow.

"No," he said.

"No?"

"No." The words left his lips with more certainty than he had felt about anything since leaving Seriphos. "I do not think so. I think the gods sent me to you for a reason. I think I am here to bring your end."

"All the men think they have been sent here to seal my fate."

"And how many of them have been given gifts by the gods to help aid them with their task?"

His heart drummed against his sternum as he awaited her reply. Whether half-god or not, many men, stronger, fitter, and better trained than him had fallen prey to the Gorgon's gaze. But he was not here to end a Gorgon's life, he realized with a sadness he could never have predicted. He was here to bring peace to a priestess.

"The sandals," Medusa said. "I'm not sure you will find them much help in severing my spine."

"But the sword of Zeus should be more than sufficient." A

shudder rolled down his spine at the casual tone of his voice. He hastened on. "And a shield too. Given to me by Athena."

Another of her now familiar scoffs made its way to his ears.

"You cannot swing faster than I can blink. My serpents will see to that. Besides, they will twist their way around any armor you have made for them."

"I do not believe it is for them. The shield, that is. I believe it is for you. For your gaze. It is a mirror that is unlike any I have encountered. Perhaps, if you were to look at it, the snakes would be confused about what they saw. It would give me a chance to strike. Only a second, but I am good with a sword." He edged closer to her voice. This was it. He was certain. This was what the gods intended for him. Not just to behead the Gorgon but to bring her story to the world. Her truth.

"I will drop the shield on the floor," he said, taking the Priestess's silence as acceptance. "If you can bend your head to look at it, only for a second, that will give me enough time to strike."

More silence followed. Outside, the storm had hastened and rain pelted to earth. Inside, the hissing had diminished to a low hum. "If you are wrong about this, I will have no choice. I will turn you to stone before you could even raise a hand against me."

"But if I am right, I will be saving both you and my mother."

"I am beyond saving," she replied. "You are not. You could turn around now and leave with your life."

He gave the comment only the briefest consideration.

"Either I leave this island with your head or not at all," he said. "Please, this will work. Let me do this for you."

TWENTY-NINE

IT WAS BUT A SECOND. A SECOND OF HOPE. A SECOND OF
sadness. She now understood why she did not speak to these
men. How much harder would it be to drag the stone statue
of the boy Perseus—loving, doting, sacrificial son—to the edge
of a cliff, knowing his mission, than it had been to drag all the
unnamed heroes that had gone before him? She would need to
remove it straightaway before her sisters returned. Who knew to
what extent they would torment her if they found a statue this
deep in their cave?

"I will throw it now," he said. "Just promise you will try."

Try. What she wanted to do was to tell him again to run. To head
back to Seriphos and save his mother with a sword and an army like
every other hero did. To forget what she had told him. But she knew
he would not listen.

With doubt and fear shadowing her heart, she heard the clang
as the mirrored shield fell to the ground and saw the flash of light
only a moment later. Her eyes and her serpent's eyes darted to
look at it.

For the first time in two thousand years, she saw herself, as clearly as all the men that had stood in front of her. The young girl, full of optimism, was long gone, although there, in the depth of her irises, she saw the slightest glimmer of hope.

EPILOGUE

FOR THE LONGEST WHILE, HE SLEPT WITH HER HEAD BENEATH his bed. It was not for fear of what his men would do with it—though that thought had crossed his mind. He kept it there for himself and the Priestess. This was her momentary sanctuary after years of torment. When he returned to Polydectes, he would find a place on Seriphos to give her the burial she deserved. That was all he could do now.

Perseus had picked his way down the rocks and back to the shore, the Kibis swollen with the mass of Medusa's head, and he had it in his mind that he would let the whole world know the truth of the Priestess. No longer would the stories told of her be tales of terror and death but rather of reverence and gratitude. The Priestess who continued to sacrifice even after death. The woman who offered herself to Perseus to save his mother from a tyrant king. So, when he boarded his ship, embraced by his men with tears in their eyes, he tried and tried again to explain that his heroism was undeserved.

Yet, every word of his protest fell on deaf ears. That first night, he learned that men did not want to hear tales of heroes who allowed a wronged priestess to sacrifice herself—unless, of course, the tale took place in a bedroom, and the priestess was half-dressed and on her knees. They did not listen as he told them of their exchange, but rather they refilled his cup and shouted over him with cheers and adulations. He realized then, alone in a crowded room, that to fulfill his promise to Medusa was to deny his loyalty to Athena, his sister, who had done all in her power to make him a hero. Telling Medusa's story would make monsters of all the men who had gone before him and failed. And what of him? Would the world respect his mercy as easily as they accepted his might and bravery?

So Perseus stayed silent. That night and every night that followed. Years passed, and Perseus went on to become one of Greece's greatest heroes, held in such high esteem for his feats. Meanwhile, Medusa's truth was lost, and all that remained was the story of monsters and heroes, though the world would never truly know which was which.

KEEP READING
FOR A LOOK AT HANNAH
LYNN'S NEXT RETELLING,
A SPARTAN'S SORROW

ONE

SWEAT WEAVED DOWN AGAMEMNON'S SPINE AS HE STUMBLED UP the rocky path. The journey had taken him longer than he had expected. There were no clouds to lessen the heat or diminish the glare of the sun, and the dry earth was crumbling beneath his feet, forcing him to keep making detours. More than once, he had struggled to maintain his footing and had been forced to crawl on hands and knees in the dust amongst the scuttling insects, until the terrain had become safer. Even the King of Kings was no match for ground like this.

Before leaving Aulis to make the journey, he had told his men that he would return in the early afternoon. Now he wondered if he would even make it back to them by nightfall. Not that it mattered. Without the guidance of the seer, their ships would be going nowhere and the mighty armada he had amassed would remain in Aulis harbor, far from the shores of Troy.

For weeks, his fleet had remained as still as paper boats on a glass pond, with not a hint of the wind they needed to take them across the Aegean Sea, to fight for Helen's return to his brother, Menelaus.

Sacrifices had been offered in the names of each of the gods: goats, sheep and enough fish to feed an entire village. But nothing seemed to satisfy them. And so, he and his fleet waited—hundreds of ships—like stagnant algae.

Stumbling again, Agamemnon cursed himself and the situation he was in. Not only was he brother to Menelaus but their wives, Clytemnestra and Helen, were sisters. His men should have been the first to land on the sands of Troy to wrest Helen from the clutches of the brazen upstart Paris. And yet, unless he could get back in the gods' good favor, they would be going nowhere. As such, this infuriating trek through parched lands was unavoidable. It was the only route to get to the seer, Calchas.

The old man was the greatest prophet in Greece, if not the world, and so it was no wonder that he kept himself to himself. Gone were the days when he would mingle with the common folk, or even take a position at a temple, nearer the towns. A man with his gifts deserved a certain level of privacy, although that didn't make the arduous journey any more agreeable. Every few steps, the King slipped on the brittle earth, the hardened skin on his feet already cracked and bleeding. Ideally, he would have brought slaves along, to carry food and water, and possibly even him. But he had been a king for long enough to know that there were some people you could impress with such displays of wealth and power and others whom you could not, and Calchas was most definitely one of the latter.

At last a small house came into view on the edge of a hill. A patch of grass shone slightly greener there, and the white walls looked clean and bright, as if they had been freshly painted that summer. As he took a moment's respite, he could have sworn he smelt the aroma of freshly baked bread drifting across to him on a warm breeze.

Whether it was real or not didn't matter as, with a new found energy, he hastened to the abode.

Filthy, tired and with his eyes stinging from the dust, he found the seer cross legged beneath a fig tree, gazing upwards toward a small flock of birds that weaved in the sky above him. The garden was simple, with fruit overburdening many of the trees, and Agamemnon was tempted to help himself to a peach or a plum to slake his thirst, but resisted the urge and moved toward the seer. Calchas's robe was draped over his arm and trailed in the dirt by his feet. Agamemnon was gratified that he had not brought his slaves with him in the end. There would be no standing on ceremony here. No formal vestments or altars bearing offerings. Not even any incense burning. Just a simple man, gifted by the gods to read the signs they gave him.

"Greetings, great Calchas." He stepped forward, casting the old man in his shadow. Moving a little to the side he cleared his throat. "Forgive the disturbance."

"It is not a disturbance." His eyes remained skyward as he spoke. "I know why you have come. You wish to learn why the winds will not take you to Troy—which god you have affronted and how you can repent."

It was a skill that was both impressive and irritating to the King. Given that the seer already knew of his need, couldn't he have sent word of what they must to do straight to Aulis? The old man had to leave this hovel of his at some point, to replenish his stores of oil and grain, if nothing else. He could easily have relayed the information then. Perhaps the gods wished that he should suffer a little first. That would be likely. Given how the insects had beset him every step of the way, he considered that sacrifice already sufficiently well met. Now all he needed to know was what type of beast he should slay, and on whose altar he should lay it.

"You are a hunter, are you not?" For the first time, Calchas's eyes left the sky and turned to Agamemnon. "You hunt all kinds of creatures."

"I am a king," he answered. "All monarchs should be able to subdue the rest of the animal kingdom. But yes, I am better than the average man with a bow and arrow."

"Is that so?"

"Well at least that is what those who wish to get in my good graces tell me." He smiled wryly to himself. He was playing the part well. Showing a level of humility. The fact was, he would challenge any man on his ship to beat him in a hunt, Achilles included. Yes, the warrior was strong and fearless, but still no match for him. There was not an animal on land that he could not track and kill, if he wanted. Before they had attempted to set sail, he had enjoyed one last hunt, through the forest of Aulis. There he had taken down a deer that had been so quick, so swift, he doubted even Artemis herself could have felled it. A fact he'd told his hunting party with pride.

"Do you recall the stag you killed?" The seer's words broke into his thoughts as if he were reading them. "That beast was sacred to the Goddess Artemis."

The words struck like ice and the heat of the day was replaced by a bitter chill that spread the length of Agamemnon's spine.

"Surely not?" he whispered. But the old man's eyes said it all. For the first time in decades, fear bloomed in the King's chest. "It was a mistake. I did not know."

"I do not doubt it."

"Then what should I do?" he asked, trying to hide the quiver in his voice, as he broke out into a cold sweat. If he did not appease the Goddess, the likelihood was that his ships would never sail at all. But the punishment for killing a sacred beast would not be insubstantial.

"A feast? A sacrifice?" he offered. "I can do both. I will kill a hundred beasts, five hundred, in her name. Tell me, what must I do? How do I seek her forgiveness?"

Without a word, the old man's gaze returned to the sky. The smallest of breezes sent a ripple through his beard, as dozens of birds took to the air once more, circling up and around toward the sun. A bitter taste burned in Agamemnon's throat as he waited to hear how much of his wealth he would have to forfeit. Calchas's gaze came back to him.

"You are a man of the gods, Agamemnon. The King of Kings, no less."

"Tell me, what is required?"

"You have faced difficult situations before, such as reclaiming your father's crown from your treacherous uncle."

"I know this. I know what I have done." His throat had grown so dry he could barely swallow. Seers should talk about the future, he thought, not drag up the past. "What is it I must do?"

The old man's eyes went back to the sky, where a single bird was hovering just a little way off in the distance. Around it, larger birds began to swoop and circle.

"She seeks only a single sacrifice," he said. "One single death on her altar in the Temple of Aulis."

Agamemnon nodded rapidly. "Yes, whatever the Goddess wishes. I will return now. I will do it this very evening."

A single death. That was straightforward enough. He just needed to know the beast. He bowed his head in respect to the seer. But when he lifted it again, the old man caught his hand.

"It is no animal she requires," he said, with a voice that could have been a thousand years old. "It is a child. Your fairest daughter, Iphigenia."

TWO

THE EVENING LIGHT LINGERED ON THE COURTYARD IN SOFT hues of tangerine and blushing pink. It was the largest in a palace full of open spaces, and had always been a favorite of Clytemnestra's. Her eldest and youngest, Iphigenia and Orestes, were sitting on a mound of cushions they had placed beneath a lime tree, feeding rabbits that hopped around their feet. Yesterday, it had been frogs from the pond, tomorrow it could be goats or chicks or whatever else they could get their hands on. Two dogs lay nearby, chewing on scraps of food that the children had given them. Sometimes she thought they would rather live on a farm, surrounded by animals, than in the palace of the great citadel of Mycenae, but that would never be. She would keep them here, by her side, for as long as was humanly possible.

The children's laughter floated on the breeze as dulcet as any tune she had ever heard. Breathing in the warm air, she leaned back in her seat and watched them play. Queen of Mycenae, a grand title but one that came with more shackles than anyone could have imagined. It was a far cry from her life in Sparta as a warrior princess—placid, mundane even. Or as mundane as was possible, when a constant veil of fear overshadowed your every move. Since her marriage to Agamemnon, her life had been divided. The public face and the private.

In private she cowered from her husband, flinching at the sight of him, knowing she had to obey his every command. She would stifle her cries, cover her bruises, and try to act as if the Clytemnestra her subjects saw was the real one. Her public face was the Queen Consort who smiled at every occasion, and dressed exquisitely in elaborate costumes that would have been an anathema in her old life in Sparta.

Even after all these years, she would find her thoughts drifting back to her homeland; to the clang of metal on metal that would accompany the evening cicada chorus, the smell of sweat ripe in the air. She remembered the fights she had won as a young girl growing up when, at only fourteen, her swordsmanship had been good enough to defeat half the boys her age, if not more. They had been so proud of her. Her father, her family—and Tantalus. With a heavy sadness, she recalled two sets of brown eyes she could lose herself in. She had been so happy. And then *he* had come.

"Orestes, you are stroking him too hard. You need to be more careful. Watch. Like this. That's better." Iphigenia took her little brother's hand and guided it gently across the rabbit's back. At two years old, Orestes was already showing himself to be far more like his elder sisters Iphigenia and Chrysothemis, than Electra. His patience, his sensitivity and his thoughtfulness were a far cry from Clytemnestra's youngest daughter, who approached every task as a potential battle and had done so practically since birth. The Queen had already found herself embroiled in more disputes with eight-year-old Electra than she had ever done with Iphigenia, who was seven years her senior.

Electra's attitude was attack first, possibly apologize later, but only if there was no alternative. Iphigenia and Chrysothemis were the opposite. Still, she worried about them all in their own way and they were what made her life in Mycenae worth living. They were the one thing that stopped her falling down the dark abyss that Agamemnon had created with his spear, all those years ago. She treasured each and every one of them, no matter what squabbles occurred.

Across the courtyard, Electra had joined her siblings, and was attempting to feed the rabbits the long stem of a dandelion, only each step she took toward them sent them scurrying under the bushes.

"You need patience, Electra," she said, rising from her seat and approaching her children. "Sit down. They will not come to you if you charge at them."

"I am not charging at them. I am trying to feed them. What kind of animals run away when you give them food? It will be their fault if they starve."

Clytemnestra smiled to herself. If any of her children belonged in Sparta, it was Electra.

"Here, sit with me," Iphigenia patted the cushion on the ground next to her. "This one is the tamest. He will let you feed him."

Electra huffed grudgingly as she dropped to the ground, her frown lifting slightly as the rabbit on her sister's lap craned out its neck to nibble the weed from her hand. When the creature finally moved across to her to finish it, Iphigenia picked up her lyre and began to play a tune. As the notes sang out, Clytemnestra closed her eyes and let her thoughts drift away. In moments like this, with her children gathered around her, she felt as though the joy of what she had might just outweigh all the terror she had suffered, and she would try to focus on what he had given her, not what he had taken away. Although she could never forget that. Nor forgive.

Time passed. She remained there, lost in the sounds of the strings and the young ones' chatter until, when the music finally stopped, she opened her eyes to find Orestes's arms bundled with three small balls of fur.

"Rabbits tired. Rabbits sleep in my bed?"

"Oh, Orestes."

"Please?"

This time she let her laughter break free. As the future king, he was the one she worried most about. His gentle nature would be remarkable enough in a girl, but to think of her son ruling the entire kingdom with such a soft heart, was enough to make her sick with worry. His kindness could be taken advantage of. He could end up succumbing to threats or being manipulated by false friendships. Or, worse still, his heart would become hardened, until that compassion had been bled from him altogether. Hopefully, with her guidance together with Agamemnon's conduct as an example of how not to behave, he would find a path somewhere between the two extremes.

"Mother?" He spoke again, having still not received an answer to his question. "Rabbits sleep in my bed?"

"What do you think your father would say to that?" she replied with a broad smile.

"He is not here," Iphigenia replied matter-of-factly. "You are the one who will have to say 'no' to him on this matter. But I do not mind. We can have the rabbits in our chamber for the night."

"I mind," Electra responded.

"Well I do not object at all," said Chrysothemis, as she lifted her head from her needlework and weighed in on the subject. "That means it is three against one."

"I suppose that means you get your way, Orestes," Clytemnestra grinned.

Despite the majority verdict, it proved far more challenging than any of them had anticipated to ferry the young rabbits from their home in the courtyard to the children's chamber. The palace extended the length of the citadel and while they had been mostly content to be picked up and carried short distances, the creatures managed to squirm their way free from their hands and make a bid for freedom several times, bounding along the marble corridors. After many screams of delight—and several more of disappointment—Clytemnestra, with the help of Iphigenia and Chrysothemis, managed to move a half dozen of the small creatures to their chamber. While Electra had relented and attempted to help, it quickly became apparent that her stomping feet and yells of frustration were more of a hindrance to their cause, so she instead went to the kitchen, to fetch them more food.

By the time they were all in bed, nightfall was well and truly upon them. The sound of dogs barking drifted through the open windows. Clytemnestra moved from one child to the next, brushing aside their hair and kissing them gently on the forehead, as she bade them goodnight. When she reached Iphigenia, her daughter sat up.

"Have you any news of father?" she asked. "I heard Orrin talking to one of the guards earlier. He said that there are still no winds. That the ships still cannot move."

"You do not need to worry about such things," Clytemnestra responded. Stroking her daughter's hair and tucking the loose strands behind her ears, she made a note to herself to talk to her Chief of Guards about discretion. Such conversations should not be held within hearing distance of her children. "The gods will bring your aunt and your father home."

"But ten years. That is what the guard said—that there is a prophecy that the war will last for ten years. Do you think it is true?

Orestes would be twelve by the time he sees Father again if that is to be believed."

Still stroking her hair, she fixed her gaze on her eldest daughter. To an outsider, Electra was the most beautiful of her children, stunning in fact. Striking and bold. But her looks were growing more severe with age, whereas Iphigenia, still only fifteen, had a fairness she had never encountered before. She would never dare utter the words out loud but she wondered if, one day, she would rival even Helen for beauty. The thought tore into her like a knife. Beauty— the most tainted gift there was. Being beautiful didn't stop a man's hands from striking you. Nor did it stop his eyes—and the rest of him—wandering when he grew tired of the same person in his bed at night. The thought of her daughters experiencing even a fraction of what she had endured, made her dizzy with fear. Before Agamemnon returned from the war, she would find Iphigenia a place in one of the Temples of Artemis. That way, she would be safe. Or as safe as any woman ever could be in this unfair world.

"A thousand rumors wash onto these shores every day," she replied to her daughter's question. "If we were to believe each of them, we would never leave the palace."

"But these are not rumors, Mother. They are prophecies. Prophecies from the gods. Prophecies from a seer are as true as the word of Zeus."

"Did *you* hear the words from the seer? Or better still, from Zeus himself?"

Her daughter pressed her lips together in thought.

"Let us talk no more of this." She smoothed down the blanket of a girl already old enough to have children of her own. "Your father will do everything right by the gods. You know this. No doubt I will have a messenger with me by morning, telling me they are already halfway to Troy. Now sleep. Tomorrow, you are going to have to help your brother clean up the mess these rabbits are making."

A motherly pride glimmered in her eyes as Iphigenia laid her head down on her pillow.

"Good night, Mother," she said.

"Good night, my love."

With the children in bed, Clytemnestra weaved her way back through the corridors and out onto the veranda, where a large carafe of wine had been placed on a table beside her seat. Next to it was a platter of dates and figs. During the day, she favored the courtyards, where a cool breeze would drift across the marble flooring but, at times like this on her own, she preferred to sit on the veranda, on the edge of the fortress. Here she would gaze out over the rolling hills, and remember.

Sometimes, if she could rouse them before sunrise, she would bring the children here too. When they were babies she would hold them to her breast and feed them as she drank in the view. With no servants or nursemaid in attendance, she could mother them as she wished. Unfortunately, although perhaps predictably, the older they grew, the less inclined they were to wake with her, particularly during the shorter days of the colder months. Apart from which, even as a small child, Electra had a penchant for danger, delighting in perching herself on the edge of the limestone wall. On more than one occasion she had feared for her daughter's life. So now, they spent most of their family time in the courtyard together, where there was more than enough room for them to run around, without her needing to worry about the perils that could befall them.

Ignoring the food, she poured herself a small cup of wine, which she cut with water, and sat back in the seat with a sigh. Ten years. She had heard the rumors of the prophecy too, and from a far more reliable source than gossiping guards. Could it really be possible? Was she really to govern Mycenae single handed for that long?

The thought was appealing. Raised as the daughter of a king, she had been accustomed to the duties of a ruler from a small child. There was even a time when she had been a queen herself. Not just an ornamental one, but a true monarch, with the promise of real power. But those days had been short lived and she knew better than to dwell on what could have been. Still, now she was to have a second chance. Who was to say Mycenae could not thrive without Agamemnon's hot temper? Of course, that and his ruthlessness were what had gained him respect. Without them, he could never have overthrown his uncle and cousin to take back the throne. He was powerful and brutal. And if, by chance or the hand of the gods, he did not return from the war in Troy, any tears she shed would be purely for show.

She was busy thinking about new ways to while away her evening hours with her husband gone—her weaving and domestic skills remained feeble, despite all the time she had spent on them— when her attention was drawn to a man waiting by the balustrade.

"Orrin," she said, beckoning him closer. "Is something wrong?"

According to the history of the citadel, he had once been one of its fiercest warriors but now his muscles had weakened with age, and the wounds he received took longer and longer to heal. Agamemnon had placed him in charge of guarding his family in his absence, rather than taking him to Troy. She knew, as such, his first loyalty lay with Orestes and yet, unlike many of the men of the citadel, he had always shown her a level of respect, which she in turn reciprocated. Ultimately, his true loyalty was to Mycenae. To its citizens and its citadel. While she would never say so out loud, she always got the impression that he did not really care who sat on the throne, as long as the people were cared for.

"There is a messenger, My Queen. He has word from the King. He will speak only to you."

She gulped down the remainder of her wine.

"Send him in. Send him to me now."

Without the need of further instruction, he disappeared back into the corridor. In just a few minutes he returned, accompanied by a man who looked as though he had traveled non-stop for several days. His coat was covered in dust and the skin on his lips was dry and flaking, while his eyes were bloodshot, as if he had gone the longest while without any rest.

"Come in. Come in." She motioned him forward, while filling a cup with water. "Drink, please. And take a seat. Then tell me what news you have of my husband. Have the winds picked up at last and sent him on his way?" *Or have the seas toppled his ship once and for all,* she silently hoped.

She extended the cup. He hesitated, before accepting and swiftly emptying the contents. The cold water brought some color back to his cheeks and, when he placed the empty vessel down, she filled it halfway with wine.

"There are no winds to sail out of Aulis," he said, "which is why I had to come to you overland."

"But did he meet with Calchas?" she questioned. "Did he find the seer?"

"He did, My Queen. He learned that it is the Goddess Artemis who has been wronged."

A cool breeze chilled her. "How?"

"I am afraid that is not of my knowledge. The King told me, however, that the Goddess has decreed a blessed union will appease her and return the winds to the sea."

"A union?" Confusion twisted her brow. Angered gods wanted

sacrifices and repentance, not blessed unions. Then again, her gripe was likely with one of the crew members and not Agamemnon himself. Perhaps she wished to repay him for the inconvenience he had suffered.

"It is your daughter, Iphigenia," he said. "You are to send her to Aulis."

"Send her to Aulis?"

The messenger's eyes finally lit up and a look of awe crossed his face. "At Aulis your daughter is to be married," he said, "to the great warrior, Achilles."

READING GROUP GUIDE

1. Despite being viewed as a feminist retelling, to what extent do you believe *Athena's Child* tackles toxic masculinity while dealing with the characters of Perseus and Dictys?

2. Why do you think Medusa was able to maintain her empathy and humanity after her transformation when her sisters no longer did?

3. How did *Athena's Child* reinforce or contradict opinions you previously had about the Greek gods?

4. Characterize Medusa and her sisters. In what ways are they similar, and how do they differ? Discuss the ways their dynamics change as the story progresses.

5. It soon becomes clear that though Perseus clamors for glory, he's simply another pawn of the gods. Would you describe him as a victim?

6. Medusa's legacy as a monster is a far-reaching one. Why do you think that is?

7. Perseus is one of the few characters who knows the injustice and cruelty of Medusa's story, yet he chooses not to share it. What did you make of this decision? Does his choice align him with the villains of this story?

8. In their final moments, both Medusa and her father feel hope. In a story like this one, do you think hope is a futile emotion? Why or why not? What is the importance of hope in even the darkest of moments?

9. Consider the blurred line between heroes and monsters in this story. Ultimately, how do we define them?

10. Medusa, like many women before and after her, is blamed and punished for her own assault. Can you draw any other parallels between this narrative and our own society?

A CONVERSATION WITH
THE AUTHOR

Greek mythology retellings, particularly those centered around female protagonists, have grown in popularity over the last decade. Why do you think this is?

Greek mythology has always been hugely popular, and so many of the well-known tales are based around male heroes. But stories told from one perspective will always be one-sided. I feel that people, myself included, want to learn more about events we feel we know so well, and that comes from hearing different viewpoints, particularly from groups that until now have been underrepresented.

With so many Greek myths, why did you choose to write Medusa's story as your first historical retelling?

Medusa is one of the most recognizable characters from all of mythology, and yet all that is commonly known about her is that she had snakes for hair and turned men to stone. Upon learning the story behind her transformation and seeing how relevant it was today, I was compelled to tell her tale in the hope that she would be remembered as more than just a monster.

How much research did you have to do before writing this book? What was the writing process like?

So much of the time I spent creating this book went into research, partly because there are different versions of Medusa's story, and it simply wasn't possible to be true to them all, due to all the variations. In the end, I used pieces from texts and myths that worked best for the version of Medusa that I wished to portray.

So many of these stories feature violence—specifically, violence against women. How do you go about navigating those topics in your writing?

They are definitely not easy to write, and being sensitive to my readers is always paramount. I never add violence into stories gratuitously and aim to focus on the mental torments as much as the physical ones, particularly the long-lasting effects of these events.

What kinds of things are you reading these days?

My reading tastes vary hugely. There are so many great retellings out there at the minute, and I love to dive back into the world of myths. Clare North's *Ithaca* was a recent standout for me, but I also enjoy all genres of stories from lighthearted rom-coms to occasional nonfiction too.

Many of these ancient stories live on because they remain relevant to us as readers or listeners. When you started writing *Athena's Child*, what parallels did you notice between Medusa's world and ours?

The great disparity in power will always, I fear, be one of the largest parallels, but there are countless others that run through Medusa's story. The way she was treated after the incident with

Poseidon is a clear one. A vulnerable young woman needed help and, instead, was turned from a victim into a perpetrator. How her sisters were punished for standing beside her also felt true of incidents within the modern world.

What do you hope readers get from this story?

I hope they feel for Medusa, and when they see the image of a woman with snakes with hair, their narrative is moved from *she was a monster who turned men to stone* to *she was a girl who was wronged and turned into a monster.*

ACKNOWLEDGMENTS

Massive thanks to my amazing editing team, including Jenna and the wonderful Carol and all my beta readers. Thank you to my husband, Jake, who has supported me constantly on this journey, and to my daughter, Elsie, who makes me want to be a better role model every day.

Lastly, thank you to every reader who has taken the time to read my work and listen to my stories, and done so much to help me along this journey. This book was such a passion project for me, so please know that every recommendation to a friend, share on social media, and kind message mean the world to me.

ABOUT THE AUTHOR

 Hannah Lynn is a multiaward-winning novelist. She published her first book, *Amendments*—a dark, dystopian speculative fiction novel —in 2015. Her second book, *The Afterlife of Walter Augustus*—a contemporary fiction novel—went on to win the 2018 Kindle Story-teller Award and the Independent Publishers Gold Medal for Best Adult Ebook.

Having lived and traveled extensively, Hannah is now settled back in the UK with her husband, daughter, and horde of cats, and spends her days writing romantic comedies and historical fiction. *Athena's Child*, which was her first historical fiction novel, was a 2020 Gold Medalist at the Independent Publishers Awards and is the first in a series of novels centered around mythological women. You can learn more at hannahlynnauthor.com.